Look what people are saying about
these talented authors

Julie Kenner

"Julie Kenner's characters and their sexual
adventures will win your heart."
—*Romantic Times BOOKreviews* on *Silent Desires*

"Kenner's steamy tale of excitement and erotica
provides immense satisfaction."
—*Romantic Times BOOKreviews* on
Silent Confessions

Karen Anders

"Karen Anders brings stimulating characters
to life with scrumptious scenes."
—*Romantic Times BOOKreviews*

"Author Karen Anders certainly knows
how to grab a reader's attention."
—*The Best Reviews*

Jill Monroe

"Hotter than a day at the beach!"
—*USA TODAY* bestselling author
Jennifer Armintrout on "Wet and Wild"

"Sizzling-hot sex, compelling characters, humor
and a dual plot make *Primal Instincts*,
by Jill Monroe, a book you can't put down."
—*Romantic Times BOOKreviews*
(Reviewers' Choice nominee)

National bestselling author **Julie Kenner** spent four years mainlining venti nonfat lattes in order to write, practice law full-time and take care of her kiddo. Then she wised up, quit the practice of law and settled down to write full-time. Her books have won numerous awards and hit bestseller lists as varied as *USA TODAY*, *Locus* magazine, Waldenbooks and Barnes & Noble. Visit Julie on the Web at www.juliekenner.com.

Karen Anders is a three-time National Readers' Choice Award finalist, *Romantic Times BOOKreviews* Reviewers' Choice finalist and has won the prestigious Holt Medallion. Karen is proud of her two daughters—one is already out in the world and the other is attending college. Although she misses the beautiful mountains of her home state of Vermont, Karen moved to northern Virginia is 1981 and then to Raleigh, North Carolina, in 2006. To contact the author, please write to her in care of Harlequin Books, 225 Duncan Mill Road, Don Mills, Ontario M3B 3K9, or visit www.karenanders.com.

Jill Monroe makes her home in Oklahoma with her family. When not writing, she spends way too much time on the Internet completing "research" or updating her blog. Even when writing, she's thinking of ways to avoid cooking. Lately Jill has happily put to use her degree in journalism with Author Talk—Where Authors Talk To Other Authors. Along with her dear friend Gena Showalter, she interviews writers, asking the questions no one else does. View these spoof interviews at www.authortalk.tv.

Julie Kenner
Karen Anders, Jill Monroe

ENDLESS SUMMER

HARLEQUIN®

TORONTO • NEW YORK • LONDON
AMSTERDAM • PARIS • SYDNEY • HAMBURG
STOCKHOLM • ATHENS • TOKYO • MILAN • MADRID
PRAGUE • WARSAW • BUDAPEST • AUCKLAND

Recycling programs for this product may not exist in your area.

ISBN-13: 978-0-373-79481-2

ENDLESS SUMMER
Copyright © 2009 by Harlequin Books S.A.

The publisher acknowledges the copyright holders of the individual works as follows:

MAKING WAVES
Copyright © 2009 by Julia Beck Kenner.

SURF'S UP
Copyright © 2009 by Karen Alarie.

WET AND WILD
Copyright © 2009 by Jill Floyd.

CONTENTS

MAKING WAVES
Julie Kenner

For Isabella

1

LACI MONTGOMERY collapsed on the sand, her entire body tingling from exertion and excitement.

She'd just ridden in on one beauty of a wave, a killer bombora that had fought her all the way in, determined to trip her up and pull her under. She'd conquered it, though, and her victory was a beauty.

"Damn," Drea said, running up the beach with Laci's video camera in her hand. "Too bad the competition hasn't started. You would have earned some serious points on that ride."

"Enough to beat you," Laci retorted, biting back a smile.

"True enough," Drea said. "Good thing the competition *hasn't* started."

"Enjoy your status while you can, rookie," Laci said, continuing the good-natured ribbing, "because I am going to totally blow you out of the water when the competition gets going."

"Smile when you say that," Drea said, aiming the camera at Laci. Laci obliged with a wide grin, then stuck her tongue out at her friend. The teasing was all in fun, and Drea knew that Laci was only playing. Well, *mostly* only playing. The truth was that Andrea Powell, Laci's friend and roommate, was the hot new thing on the female surfing circuit, the rookie of the year who was usually the subject of the cameras. Laci and Drea had only known each other a few weeks, but they'd bonded fast, and Laci genuinely wished Drea all the best. Well, mostly the best. Because if Laci had her way, Drea was about to be seriously outclassed by the new girl in town: Laci Montgomery, this year's wild-card entry in the Girls Go Banzai surfing competition.

"You're going down, girlfriend," she said, but with a smile.

"Am I?" Drea said as she pointed toward the surf. "Or are we both going to get our asses seriously kicked?"

Drea's finger was aimed right at JC Wilcox, a world-class surfer with the trophies to prove it. Laci would have had to hate her if JC wasn't such a great friend. She contented herself with being annoyed at JC's habit of leaving her towel draped over the curtain rod in the one-bathroom bungalow the three of them were sharing until after the competition.

"She's looking really good," Laci said with mixed envy and pride. She and JC had been friends for over a year, and during that time, Laci had learned a lot about JC. Mostly, she knew that the Hawaiian-born beauty was one hell of a surfer, and she deserved all her accolades and honors, but right then, JC had what Laci coveted: an actual corporate sponsor.

She sighed, telling herself it was the steady income of a sponsorship that she wanted. However, that wasn't entirely true. She could always find a way to make money, JC's trophies and sponsorships meant more than a paycheck. They meant that JC had earned her place in surfing.

And so far—although Laci had busted her tail and had some solid accolades and competitions under her belt—Laci still didn't have the holy grail. She still didn't have validation. And so help her, she craved it.

"You okay?" Drea's head was cocked, examining Laci's face.

"I'm fine." In fact, she wasn't. She was desperate for a win; desperate to prove herself here at Banzai. And that fierceness in her left a guilty hole in her stomach. But she couldn't help it— she wanted to win. Wanted it and needed it.

More than that, she was certain that Drea and JC wanted it, too. But that was the kind of thing the girls didn't talk about unless they disguised it as joking. Sure, they were friends. But hanging out on the beach and discussing their pasts and their boyfriends and their surfboard wax was one thing. Copping to the hope of unseating both of her friends and taking a world-class championship? Well, that was an *unspoken* given, with unspoken being the key operating word.

Tease about it, yes.

Seriously state out loud that you want to beat your friend? Just not done.

But Laci wanted it. Oh, yeah. She wanted it bad.

"You don't look fine," Drea said. "Are you nervous?"

"A little," Laci admitted. "I'm still in a bit of shock, I think. I mean, I'm in Hawaii, competing in one of the hottest competitions on the planet. I've seen my picture on the Internet and in the local paper, and when we go into the bars and diners, the waitstaff actually knows my name. It's—"

"A trip," Drea said.

"Disconcerting," Laci countered. More than that, all this unanticipated press was exactly the reason she was so anxious to prove herself. She was the wild card in this competition—here because she was plucked out of the pile of all the potential surfers by XtremeSportNet, the corporation that was hosting and sponsoring the Girls Go Banzai competition here in Hawaii.

Most of the competitors had arrived at the competition through what Laci thought of as the usual route. In other words, they had entered a less prestigious, more locally oriented contest that fed into a bigger contest that fed into a *bigger* contest, until finally the top-ranking surfers in a dozen or so competitions were eligible to compete at Banzai.

In contrast, Laci hadn't played the competition circuit. Instead, she'd been invited by the sponsor—XtremeSportNet—to compete at Banzai as a wild card, which traditionally meant that the sponsor had seen the surfer at exhibitions or other competitions, had liked what they saw, and thought the wild card would be an asset to the overall competition.

She scowled, thinking of all the possible ways a sponsor might consider a surfer an asset. Media appeal, for example. But Laci was interested in none of that, and now that she was here, she figured it was her job to prove to everyone that she was picked because of her skill and only her skill.

Drea's eyebrows rose. "What's eating you?"

"Let's just say I don't get it," Laci said. "It's not like I've won anything yet, so what's the big deal? All this attention. It feels like I'm getting something for nothing." And that scenario grated on Laci. Always had. Always would. "I didn't even go through the trials." She'd been in Australia tending to her little sister after a car accident. The accident had been minor, but Laci had practically raised Millie, and not even the trials for Girls Go Banzai was going to keep her from Millie's side.

"Big deal. It wasn't like you've been blowing off surfing or losing your edge. You've been doing exhibitions and contests nonstop for the last fourteen months. Ever since you backed out of San Clemente."

Laci licked her lips. That one stung.

Drea glanced at her sideways. "So I'm thinking that you've got something to prove."

"Maybe," Laci admitted.

Drea studied her, then nodded. "Well, obviously it worked. They only bring in girls who deserve it as wild cards, and that would be you."

"Deserve it," Laci repeated, her mind drifting back to San Clemente, a highly touted but very new addition to the competition circuit run by one of XtremeSportNet's competitors. She'd been brought in as a wild card there, too, and she'd been foolishly, stupidly giddy about it. At least she had until she heard the rumors that she'd slept her way into the competition, trading sex for a slot. And no matter how much she denied them, the insinuations wouldn't go away. Why would they, when her then-boyfriend was Taylor Dutton, the man who'd been in charge of promoting that competition?

He'd denied it, of course, but considering that the media was already all over the story and her reputation was shot, nothing he said made a whit of difference.

The trouble, of course, was that she'd trusted him. No, more than that; she'd *loved* him. They'd been dating on and off for two months, and they'd fallen into a pattern of easy familiarity that had tingled around the edges. Simply sitting next to each other at a table eating breakfast cereal had moved her, and he could turn her to mush with a soft brush of his thumb against her cheek as easily as with a deeply passionate embrace and a slow slide into bed.

She'd loved him and she'd trusted him, and because she had, the hurt had gone that much deeper when the media broke the big story that he'd pulled the strings to get her into the competition as a coveted wild-card contender. Not because she deserved it, which she did, thank you very much, but because she'd been sleeping with him.

She'd wanted to dump him in a flurry of curses and flying pieces of furniture, but instead she'd dumped him with a quiet fury she liked to think was elegant and controlled. Then she'd scurried away to lick her wounds and tell herself that if she never saw Taylor Dutton again, it would be too soon.

For a few weeks there, she'd even considered leaving surfing behind, but then JC had kicked her butt and told her to get out there on the circuit and prove that Laci didn't have to sleep her way to a trophy or a world ranking—she could surf her way there just fine.

As surfing competitions went, San Clemente wasn't yet a blip on the world-class radar. So her surfing career hadn't taken too much of a hit when she'd backed out, in spite of all the local media attention. Even so, there was no way—*no way*—she'd been willing to hang in there and let people think that sex had eased her entry into the events. And for the next fourteen months, she'd aimed for the gold standard—highly prestigious competitions. Competitions that could kick a girl up into the world rankings. Competitions that could get her noticed and get her a sponsor.

Girls Go Banzai was one of those competitions, and even if Millie's accident had meant that she'd missed the primary feeder competition for Banzai, nothing changed the fact that Laci had spent weeks carefully selecting which competitions and exhibitions she surfed. She'd done her best, busted tail on the waves, and she'd gotten herself noticed.

Herself. Not her former jerkwad of a bed partner.

So, yeah. She deserved this wild-card spot. And with a quick "I absolutely, totally do deserve it," she told Drea so.

"Well, there you go," Drea said, as if that solved everything. Laci sighed. Maybe it did.

Besides, once she won, that queer, uncomfortable feeling would go away. No one could say that she hadn't earned the attention (or, she hoped, the endorsements) because the trophy would be sitting on her mantel. But until she actually won, she was just a pretender. And that was a role that didn't sit well with Laci at all.

"Is Millie coming?" Drea asked, shifting the subject to Laci's little sister.

Laci shook her head. "I wish. But she's in Sydney doing *The Magic Flute*. A small role, but she's got a solo, and she totally steals the show." The car accident, thank goodness, hadn't slowed Millie's career one iota.

"Really? That's awesome. You must be totally proud."

"Enough to bust a gut," Laci admitted, though Drea didn't know the half of it. The truth was, Laci had been more like a mom to Millie than like a sister. No one knew the full story because Laci had never felt close enough to anyone to share. Couple that with the fact that dredging up her sub-par childhood was not on Laci's list of fun things to do, and it made for a topic that was definitely not discussed in polite conversation.

She'd never even shared the details of her childhood with Taylor. He'd known she was close to her sister, of course. But all the other baggage… That stuff was best left buried.

Drea whipped the towel from around her hips and laid it out on the sand, then settled in, faceup to the sun, the pink zinc oxide on her nose making her look cuter than usual.

Laci swallowed a frown as she settled back, towelless, on the sand. Next to Drea and JC, she'd always felt plain. Brownish-blond hair, a smattering of irritating freckles and a mouth she'd always considered too big. *Fresh,* the press was calling her now, which Laci interpreted as code for "not sexy in the least." Not that it mattered. She was here to surf, not to win a beauty pageant.

Besides, the press chatter about her looks was a lot better than the alternative. So far, at least, not one reporter had mentioned the San Clemente scandal. As far as Laci was concerned, it couldn't get much better than that.

Drea turned her head, opened her eyes and frowned. "Do you want to share my towel?"

She squirmed a little, digging her heels into the warm sand, enjoying the feel of the grains against her back and legs. "No thanks." The sensation teased her, reminded her of what she was there for and of how far she'd come. All the way from her screwed-up childhood in Laguna Beach, California, where she wasn't allowed to take a towel to the beach because her mom didn't want to risk tracking any bit of grit or grime into their blindingly white, paid-for-with-other-people's-money beach-front condo.

All of that hadn't mattered then, and it didn't matter now. Laci had grabbed Millie's hand and marched the two of them jauntily through the glitz-and-marble lobby. They'd crossed the walking path to the dunes and plunked themselves down on the sand, Laci's six years on this earth qualifying her for elder-statesman status over her four-year-old sister. The California beaches weren't warm like the ones in Hawaii, but to this day she could remember the smell of the surf, and she could still feel the suction beneath her toes as she wiggled them in the warm, wet sand.

They'd stay outside as long as they could, cooking under a layer of sunscreen, and cooling off with quick dips in the surf and slushies from Joe who worked the concession shack. Then they'd traipse back to the condo, only to be waylaid by Manuel, the doorman, who'd invariably tell her that her mom had a "special guest," and suggest that Laci and Millie get cleaned up in the poolside shower and maybe take a quick swim for, oh, another thirty-five minutes.

Millie was too young to understand, but even at six, Laci got it: stay out of their mom's way for a while longer, and by the next day, they'd have a few new clothes, food in the fridge and a mother who wasn't in a perpetually pissy mood. Usually, Laci scored a new toy—which she immediately dropped in the charity box at the grocery store, though she'd never, ever tell her mother for fear of one of Alysha's famous spankings. Their mom had a temper, no doubt about that. And woe be to any adult or child who looked askance at the way she provided for her kids.

It had been a surreal kind of life, all the more so during the school year when the other moms would pull their daughters away from Laci and Millie, whispering to their girls about associating with the "wrong sort." Laci didn't want to be wrong, and she hated the fact that her mother took and took and took, getting by on looking pretty and having the men fawn all over her. She hadn't known it at the time, of course, but Alysha Montgomery had been the worst kind of whore, trading on her looks, doling out sex and not doing one damned thing to earn herself a place in the world.

Alysha had never crossed the line into out-and-out prostitution, but she'd certainly been "kept." And when Child Protective Services started poking around to investigate how well she was looking after her two young daughters, Alysha had decided that her girls weren't worth fighting for and had insisted their father come from Australia to pick them up.

Laci had been terrified at first by the prospect of going off to live with a man she didn't remember. Then the reality sank in: she was getting to leave her leech of a mother. And no matter what else happened, that had to be a good thing.

Fortunately, she'd been right. Moving from her mom's dolled-up condo to her father's ramshackle shack had constituted serious culture shock, but Duncan had made them feel more welcome in two days than their mom had in their entire lives. Without breaking stride, he'd brought his daughters into his life, and he'd never once complained, even though two little girls had taken up more than their fair share of his four-hundred-square-foot shack.

They'd arrived during the summer, and while Duncan had sat at the lifeguard stand, his daughters played in the surf and got to know the vendors who hawked food, air rafts and surfboards to the locals and tourists.

By the end of that first summer, Laci had learned to surf, and three months later—during their first Christmas/summer break

Down Under—she'd competed in her first surfing competition, coming out of nowhere to take second in the junior division.

After that, she knew what she'd wanted to do for the rest of her life, and she'd gone after her goal with single-minded obsessiveness. Her first surfboard had been a present from her father, but after that, she'd eschewed trading product for favors. No way—no freaking way—was she turning into her mom.

She intended to climb to the top of the surf world, win trophies and world championships and get her face on cereal boxes. And she was getting there on her own merits—her own wins. Or, dammit, she wasn't getting there at all.

"Thinking serious thoughts?" That comment came from JC, now standing over Laci and blocking the sun, so that the backlight through her damp hair made her appear like some sort of Amazon surf goddess.

"Always," Laci said, pushing up on her elbows and conjuring a smile.

Beside her, Drea rolled over, joining the conversation. "You looked good out there," she said, and Laci nodded agreement.

"Thanks," JC said, plunking down on the sand beside them. "Hard to believe the first heat's in just two weeks. I'm totally digging this relaxation time."

Laci laughed. "Some relaxation! We're working our tails off."

"Okay, you have a point."

"Should we say it now," Drea asked. "Just to get it out of the way?"

They looked at each other, then each grinned as they stuck out their hands, putting one on top of the other. "Good luck," they said in unison. "But I'm gonna kick your ass." They tossed their hands in the air and fell back, laughing.

Nice to laugh about it, Laci thought. She wondered if the others meant it even half as much as she did.

JC climbed to her feet. "I'm going to go grab a shower and some lunch. You guys?"

"Sure," Drea said, shaking out her towel and securing it back around her hips. "Laci?"

Laci shook her head, the thought of spending some alone time on the beach too enticing to pass up. "I'm going to hang here for a while, but I might swing by Da Kine later for a snack. You want me to call you?"

"Sure," Drea said, and although JC nodded, there was a shadow in her eyes.

"What?" Laci demanded.

"It's probably nothing," JC said.

"Then spit it out."

"It's just that when I was in there last night, I thought I saw someone. I'm not even sure. It's probably nothing."

Laci was bolt upright now, her back straight, senses tingling. "Who did you see?"

"*Thought* I saw," JC clarified.

Laci crossed her arms and stared down her friend.

"Fine. I thought I saw Taylor Dutton."

Drea let out a low whistle even as Laci's insides went cold. "Here? Working the competition? That doesn't make any sense. He doesn't even work for Xtreme."

Drea and JC exchanged looks. "Yeah, he does," JC said. "Has been for a while, actually. But," she hurried to add, possibly because she saw panic on Laci's face, "there's no way I could have seen him. I mean, he doesn't have any reason to be here," JC said. "Morgan Castle's here for Xtreme. I talked to him yesterday." She waved a hand, as if dismissing the whole conversation. "It was probably someone who looked like Taylor. I shouldn't have said anything."

"No," Laci said. "It's okay. Taylor doesn't mean a thing to me anymore. For that matter, he never meant anything. He was a fling. That's all."

They both looked at her as if they didn't believe her, which made sense considering she was lying through her teeth.

"Go on," she said. "I'm gonna hang for a while and then go back to the bungalow. And don't look so stricken. I'm fine. He's not even really here, right? And I can totally handle bumping into someone who vaguely looks like a guy I dated a while ago. Really," she added because her friends still seemed dubious.

Despite their obvious hesitations, they finally left, but not before making her promise to call if she needed anything.

She wouldn't.

Even if Taylor were on the island—and why would he be with Morgan gunning to score big promoter points with his boss?—it wasn't as if Laci were still pining for the guy. Yes, she'd been blindsided before, but she'd wised up a lot since then. She'd confused pheromones for love and she'd gotten seriously burned as a result, her surfing triumphs tainted with the sour stench of sex traded for prime publicity ops. *Sodding scumbag.*

She'd left him on the beach in California and she'd never looked back.

Laci was *not* like her mom. Everything she had, she'd earned. And now here she was at Girls Go Banzai, a competition that she'd only dreamed about, and certainly hadn't hoped to achieve so soon. And, as Drea had said, XtremeSportNet saw potential in her, when they picked her as the Banzai wild card, and she was going to make sure they also saw a star.

Of course, for that to happen, she had to get up off this beach. And right at this moment, with the sun beating down on her, that seemed like the hardest thing in the world.

With a sigh, she wriggled deeper into the sand and said a silent thank-you that the first heat of the competition was still weeks away. JC was right—even though they had work to do in these upcoming weeks, relaxation was definitely on the agenda. Laci loved Hawaii, and although she intended to practice within an inch of her life, she also wanted to chill. Because in the end, the stereotypes were true: a laid-back, loose surfer would do way better in competition than a surfer wound tight as a spring.

And the news of Taylor's possible presence on the island had definitely wound her up.

She just needed a few more minutes to let the sun and sand work their magic on her muscles.

Feeling utterly decadent, she arched her foot, then pressed her toes under the top layer of warm sand to the cool, wet mush below. The change in temperature shot through her, and that combined with the warm sun on her belly and breasts sent a sensual trill through her body.

She breathed deeply, enjoying the sensation and enjoying more the fact that she'd gotten here on her own. Taylor Dutton might have been an A-1 ass, but she'd kicked him firmly to the curb. She was here on this island in this competition because she'd earned it. Earned this sand. Earned this chance. And she intended to enjoy it.

"Heaven," she whispered, her word coming out on a soft breath.

"Looks like it from here," came the response in a deep, masculine drawl filled with Southern charm and ripe amusement.

Laci's eyes flew open, and she found herself staring up into the ice-blue gaze of the one man she'd hoped never to see again.

The man who'd screwed her over.

The man who'd ruined her reputation.

And yes, the man she'd loved with all her heart and soul. *Taylor Dutton.*

2

NICE TO KNOW some things never changed, Taylor thought as he took the brunt of Laci's wrath. Her fiery temper—not to mention the sexy gleam in her eye—was exactly as he'd remembered it. And exactly what he'd been missing.

Laci Montgomery had gotten under his skin last year, and he'd never managed to shake her loose, despite the fact that she hated him for something he hadn't even done. The machinations, sure. But how the hell was he supposed to know that the press would jump to the conclusion that the only reason she was a featured exhibition participant was because they were sharing a bed? It had been his job to find exciting new talent for the competition, and he'd fallen head over heels for the sexiest, most exciting woman that he'd ever run across on the surf circuit.

Yeah, he'd fallen in love with her.

And yeah, he'd wanted the whole world to fall in love with her, too.

So he'd brought her in as a wild-card contestant, and it was just their bad luck that some idiot reporter looking for a headline realized they'd been dating. But so what? It wasn't as if Laci didn't know her way around a board. She was absolutely brilliant on the waves.

He'd told her not to worry about it—he'd even managed to get the press to focus on her skills and rocketlike climb up through the surfing ranks. But like a dog with a bone, they'd refused to drop the sex angle.

And, okay, maybe it was his fault for mentioning to a reporter that they were dating, but he'd only said it because he was so proud of her. Laci, however, hadn't seen it that way, especially after the press had jumped all over the story. And because of that, Laci dropped him. In her mind, since he'd been in charge of the media relations for the competition, he took the blame for their rabid reporting. As if he'd intentionally leaked them a hot story.

As if he hadn't been falling head over heels in love with her when she'd yanked the rug right out from under him.

He'd been pissed—no, he'd been furious—and she'd added fuel to his already raging fire when she'd walked out on both him and the competition, leaving a hole in his heart and a chip on his shoulder. He'd been angry ever since. Angry at himself for mishandling the entire situation, and angry at Laci for not having guts enough to face the press and tell them to take a flying leap. Her surfing was what had gotten her into the exhibition, and anyone with two eyes on the waves could tell that just by looking at her perform.

She'd never even tried to defend her skill, though, and that was the one thing he'd never understood. It gnawed on him, especially since running away hadn't changed the Big, Bad Media's opinion. Just the opposite, actually. Her knee-jerk reaction had only increased the speculation that she'd used sex to get her name on the exhibition roster in the first place.

He'd been smug at first, figuring it served her right for being so cavalier with his heart. Then the anger had faded, and he owned up to being a major jerk. The truth was, he'd pulled her in because she was a damn good surfer, and as a newbie promoter with the responsibility of helping to launch a new competition, he needed as many damn good surfers as he could get. And it didn't hurt if the surfers were camera-friendly, which Laci certainly was.

And yes, he'd picked her because she was his girlfriend. At the time, he'd believed he was doing her a favor—getting her name out there and her talent on display.

It had never occurred to him that the media would insinuate that she'd landed her position in the competition by sleeping with him. He'd been blindsided—he could admit that now—and he hadn't handled the situation well at all.

In fact, not only had he not handled it well, but he hadn't handled her at all. He'd basically told her to buck up, and never once had he simply let her cry on his shoulder. He'd been The Promoter, not The Boyfriend, and that failure, along with all his other mistakes, had killed their relationship.

But even now—even knowing all that—he still didn't understand why she hadn't fought back. Why hadn't she made a statement or ignored the media or just shown any backbone at all? What he did know was that he'd been a major player in making her hurt.

And didn't that feel just dandy in his heart?

For months, he'd wanted to call her, but he'd been too afraid of getting slapped down again. So he'd stayed away, silently watching her climb back through the ranks, her reputation soaring as her skill on the waves outshone the stench of bad media and cruel rumors.

But as they both moved deeper and deeper into the surfing circuit, keeping his distance was proving to be difficult. Especially with Reginald Pierce riding him.

The truth was, Taylor was truly grateful to Reggie. The owner of XtremeSportNet, Reggie had called Taylor into his corner office last week and asked if he'd booked his flight for Hawaii.

Taylor had shaken his head, baffled. "I'm not even going to Hawaii," he'd said, though he half wished he was. She would be there, after all, and a piece of his soul longed to see Laci again. "Morgan has the ball on that. I'm heading down to Sydney to get things in place for Danger." The Danger Down Under event was a brand-new competition that XtremeSportNet had dreamed up, and against all odds, Reggie had decided to put Taylor in the driver's seat. As assignments went, if Taylor could pull it off, this one would ensure that his career was destined for top management.

Taylor most definitely intended to pull it off. And in a big, big way.

He had his media lined up, his cosponsors and his headlining surfers. So Taylor couldn't imagine why Reggie wanted him to waste even a minute in Hawaii when he needed to be at the far end of the Pacific.

But where Reggie was concerned, Taylor had learned to trust first and ask questions later. After all, Reggie had plucked him away from a competing company only one month after Taylor had worked San Clemente. Reggie had said that he saw a spark in Taylor, a spark that needed room to burn, and Taylor had been working his way up the XtremeSportNet ranks for the last year.

At this rate, he'd be working at corporate headquarters before his thirtieth birthday.

Since coming onboard with XtremeSportNet, all of Taylor's dreams were coming true. The Georgia boy who'd grown up without a penny to his name now had a full-to-popping bank account. Money, respect and a solid career path—everything he'd craved. Everything his parents had never had, and it was all right there at his fingertips. All he had to do was keep his job.

All he had to do was keep Reggie happy.

And if keeping Reggie happy meant that Taylor had to suffer the horrors of a meeting in beautiful, exotic Hawaii…well, there were worse things a boss could ask a guy to do.

It wasn't until Taylor set foot on the island that Reggie slipped an ulterior motive his way, insisting that Taylor "make nice" to "our wild-card gal."

Taylor had blinked, and his confusion must have shown on his face, because Reggie had leaned forward across his desk. "Any bad blood that's left between you two, you clear it away. I want it gone by the time Banzai starts. You got that?"

"I got it," Taylor had replied, though it had been difficult to talk with his back teeth clenched together. "You want to tell me why?" He couldn't think of a single reason why Reggie would care if Taylor and Laci were on speaking terms. And unless there was a damn good one, he resented the hell out of being pulled off his own assignment.

Reggie leaned back and steepled his fingers in front of him. "I'm not inclined to explain myself to employees, Dutton. But I like you, and I think you've got a big future ahead of you. So let me simply say that I don't believe a competition can thrive if there's bad blood. And I want Danger Down Under on Laci's dance card. But if she's looking at that opportunity with eyes that think you're lower than slime, well…" He trailed off with an exaggerated shrug of his shoulders.

"And you think we have to deal with this now?" Taylor asked. "The slate for the first Danger competition's already lined up, and Laci isn't on it. I should be there dealing with details, not hanging in Hawaii to thwart a potential future problem." His words were firm, but he worked hard to keep the anger out of his voice. And yeah, he was angry, because Reggie's reasons were ridiculous. And every day Taylor was away from Sydney meant that his assistant—an overeager little Chihuahua of a woman named Darlene—developed the relationships he needed to be stroking. "Why not worry about it later?"

"I'm not a big fan of procrastination," Reggie had said. "If she wins the Hawaii competition, I want her hyped up to agree right then and there for every other competition we sponsor. I don't want her hesitating over hurt feelings. Okay, Taylor?"

Taylor nodded.

But despite the frustration of Reggie's motives and plan, Taylor had to admit that he liked where he'd ended up. And now—standing over her like he was—he thought he ought to send Reggie a box of cigars as a thank-you gift. Because this was the kick in the pants he'd needed to make up for the past and dream about the possibility of a future with Laci.

That might not be Reggie's agenda, but right now, that wasn't something Taylor was worried about. Right now, all he wanted to do was see that smile of Laci's that had filled his thoughts on the flight from Los Angeles. He'd imagined walking up to her and telling her in words so brutally honest they were poetic, that he'd missed her. And she'd smile at him and hold out her hand.

He studied her expression now and realized that his dreams were bullshit, and that if he wanted her back, he was going to have to bust his tail going after her. Because considering the scowl on Laci's beautiful face, she sure as hell wasn't sliding into his arms anytime soon.

"What are you doing here?" she asked.

"It's a public beach," he answered, then immediately kicked himself. Defensive and irritated wasn't the right way to play this. He didn't want to be *playing* at all.

"You have some serious balls showing up here and talking to me," she said, her eyes flashing with the same passion he'd seen in his bed, only this time the fire was fueled by hate and not desire.

Pettiness twisted his gut. Like a fool in love, he'd harbored secret fantasies of her wanting him back. Foolish, childish fantasies.

Fantasies, he realized now, that would never come true.

"Balls of steel," he said, standing a little bit straighter as he shifted his perspective on the world.

Her eyes darted away, and he saw the tiniest hint of a frown touch her lips before she looked up at him. "I guess I know better than anyone. You were all steel when I left, weren't you? Not a soft spot anywhere."

As he cringed, she hauled herself up out of the sand, then peered at her waterproof watch. "Oh, gee. Time to go," she said, her chin held high, her posture perfect. She looked like Aphrodite with the ocean turning to foam behind her and the sun glowing on her copper-colored skin. Bits of sand clung to her, and his fingers itched to touch her, to brush the grains away and feel the soft skin beneath. Laci was grace and strength combined, and seeing her now drove home just how much he'd lost when she'd walked out of his life.

"You want to get out of my way?" she demanded. "It's getting crowded out here."

He noted the completely empty beach. "Wait," he said, reaching for her hand. He told himself that he was only there to make nice with Laci and ensure his own job security. Any illusions about getting back together with her had been cut off at the knees by the vitriol he'd seen in her eyes.

He told himself that, but it wasn't true. He wanted to touch her. *Had* to touch her. And now that her arm was cupped inside his palm, he knew the instinct had been right. Her skin was warm and soft, and she trembled slightly under his touch, letting his hand linger for longer than it needed to before she tugged her hand away, her cheeks glowing, and not from the sun.

His heart skipped in his chest, the band that had settled around it loosening. He had a chance here, his heart was saying. Dear God in heaven, he actually still had a chance with her.

She started to walk away, and he fell into step beside her. "Dammit, Taylor," she said.

"Just two folks going in the same direction."

She stopped, turned to him with her hands on her hips. "What? What do you want from me?"

"What makes you think I want anything from you?"

"Are you saying you don't?"

"No," he admitted. "I do."

"All right, then. What?"

"Dinner," he said, then watched, amused, as pure astonishment filled her clear blue eyes.

"Dinner," she repeated.

"That's all. Eating. Drinking. Talking. We've done all three before, and had a good time doing it. Had a good time after, too, if I remember right."

"You're such a jerk." She started walking away, and he kicked himself for going too far. That was the way he'd always been around her—his defenses dropped, and he spoke his mind more than he ever had around a woman. He'd assumed that time, distance and the utter destruction of their relationship would have cured him of that defect, but apparently not.

"Laci, wait." He hurried to catch up, positioned himself right in front of her so that she had to either stop or go around. He held his breath, exhaling only when she stopped. *Yup. Definitely a chance here.*

"Why?" she demanded.

"Do I need a reason?"

"You've come a long way," she said. "So, yeah. I'm thinking you need a reason."

"I want to make it up to you," he answered.

She stared at him as if he'd grown horns. "Excuse me?"

"Dammit, Laci," he said, the frustration that had been building in him for the last fourteen months coming to a head now that she was finally in front of him. "We were good together, and it ended badly. Whether that was my fault or your fault doesn't matter anymore."

"The hell it doesn't."

"Fine. I messed up. Can I buy you dinner? Can I try to make it up to you? I'm not even working the competition, Lace."

He could see the curiosity—and the interest—sparking in her eyes, and he felt guilt twinge in his stomach. He'd spoken the truth, but that didn't change the fact that he hadn't exactly laid all the facts at her feet.

"Why exactly are you in Hawaii?" she asked, getting to the heart of the matter, not to mention the meat of his guilt.

"I came because you're here," he replied, which was another completely honest answer with a hole in it so big it rivaled the Chunnel.

"Because of me," she repeated. Not a question, but a statement, her voice flat, as if she were trying to find some place in the reality of her life where his words actually made sense. "And you're not working Girls Go Banzai?"

He shook his head. "That's Morgan's baby. I'm based in Sydney right now. Putting together the Danger Down Under competition." He saw her reaction, and wasn't at all surprised. Danger Down Under had already generated buzz in the surfing world, and was shaping up to be a can't-miss competition.

"Long way from Sydney," she said.

"Not really. I'm calling it a long layover." He stepped closer, shoving his hands into his pockets so he wouldn't reach for her hands. She met his eyes, and he smiled. "The truth is, I wasn't going to pass up the chance to see you again."

The corner of her mouth quirked, both amused and suspicious. "Chance? I haven't exactly fallen off the planet, Taylor. And last I checked, my cell phone number was the same. The last year has been filled with any number of chances," she added, nailing him with that too-smart-for-her-own-good glare. "So why now?"

His gut twisted once again, and he knew he couldn't lie to her any more than he could tell her the whole truth. He searched her eyes for some clue that if he laid his heart on the line, the risk would pay off. But he saw nothing there. Which meant he had to go out on a limb. Standard operating procedure in his job, but not so much in his personal life.

"Why?" she pressed.

He closed the distance between them until he could smell the ocean on her skin, the heat from her body sufficient to drive him crazy. "Because I haven't been able to get you out of my mind," he admitted. "Because I wanted you the first day I saw you, and nothing has changed. Because I still remember the way your skin felt beneath my hand. And," he added, hearing her soft intake of breath, "because there was no other choice. I simply had to come."

3

LACI FELT her heart flutter and tried to stay in control. He *had* to come? After all this time? After she'd gotten her head back on straight and recovered from the wound he'd left?

Now he had to come?

A wave of anger overtook her, but common sense stayed her hand before she reached out and slapped him across the cheek. She wanted to—oh, how she wanted to. He'd hurt her so badly.

And the absolute hell of it? Even while she stood there wanting to slap him, a larger part of herself—the desperate, needy, traitorous part—wanted to move into his arms and feel them close tightly around her. She wanted the scent of him on her and his breath in her ear as he whispered soft words.

She wanted all that, but there was no way she was going to have it. No way she'd give him the satisfaction.

Schooling her expression into one of calm diffidence, she tilted her head back and looked up into his eyes. She tried to say something, but couldn't find the words. He'd twisted her heart and her thoughts into too much of a tangle.

And so she simply held his gaze, her teeth clenched so tightly together her jaw ached. And then she turned her back on him and marched calmly toward the surf.

She knew his eyes were on her, and the hardest thing in the world she had ever done was not to look back. And she wanted so badly to see the expression on his face. Worse than that, she wanted to run to him.

Pathetic, Laci. You're absolutely pathetic.

And she was *so* not going there. She was doing just fine without Taylor Dutton in her life, thank you very much. Last time she checked, she had absolutely no masochistic tendencies, and now was not the time to start clinging to a man who was clearly bad for her.

She grabbed her board from where she'd left it a few feet up from the surf line and tucked it under her arm. Then she jogged a ways into the water before putting it down and positioning herself on top.

She paddled out, her arms working automatically, which was a good thing, as her mind was still on what had happened on the beach.

Bad for me. He was bad, bad, bad for me.

Except, was he?

Stop it, Laci. Do not go there.

She frowned. Yes, he'd betrayed her trust, and yes, that was about as bad as it got. But before that…

Well, before that, he'd been the best thing that had ever happened to her.

Betrayal trumps soul-mate status, doofus. Just because you're starved for sex doesn't mean you need to run back to the likes of Taylor Dutton. He sucked you in, remember? And that made the hurt all the worse.

Clearly, paddling out had been a bad idea. She'd always had the habit of talking to herself in the water. Usually her conversations leaned more toward reminding herself to find her center, or to wait for the next wave, or to comment on another surfer who had the potential to show Laci up.

Today, her chatty alter ego was all about the guy.

She supposed that was to be expected, especially since everything the voice in her head was saying was true. But even so, she couldn't help but remember the long walks at night with Taylor. The talks they'd had until the wee hours of the morning. Talks about nothing, and yet somehow those talks had been everything. Because with Taylor, it hadn't been all about the sex. There'd been a connection. A caring. *A bonding.* Something she hadn't felt before and hadn't experienced since.

She missed it. Honestly, she missed him.

Bad. Bad, Laci.

With an extreme force of will, she shoved thoughts of Taylor out of her head and concentrated on the ocean, the swell and the pull of the current. As a rule, surfing was a safe sport, but there were risks in all activities, especially at her level. For that matter, she knew better than to go out on the waves by herself. But Taylor had messed with her head, and she needed it. Needed the water and the waves and the freedom. And yeah, she needed the rush to fight the burn of rampant sexual energy.

She'd be careful and easy and take it slow, but she sure wasn't turning back.

This beach was away from the Pipeline where she'd be surfing in competition, but even so, the waves normally rocked. They certainly had only hours earlier when Drea had been out here with her.

Part of that, of course, was the result of swells brewing with the coming storm. Area meteorologists had been watching cells for days, and the consensus was that a doozy would blow in that evening. Now, in fact, the ocean had calmed a bit—the clichéd calm before the storm. Laci didn't care about the reason for the calm, but for the first time in her surfing life, she was actually grateful for the lame waves, because right then, she could only keep half her mind on the water. The other half kept dancing back to Taylor, damn his dark and evil soul.

She scowled and focused, doing a neat duck dive under the incoming waves. She wasn't out far enough yet, and although the conditions were slacking, she still hoped for a sweet ride back.

Emerging from under the wave, she blinked the water out of her eyes and tasted the salt on her mouth, enjoying the little slice of heaven. She felt more at home on the waves than she'd ever felt anywhere in her life, with the sad exception of Taylor's arms. She chalked *that* up to girlish stupidity, however. Taylor wasn't home. Or rather, if he was, he was just like the home her mother had made.

And that was no home at all.

Although Laci had to admit she owed the woman big-time. After all, if her defective excuse for a maternal unit hadn't decided to dump Laci and Millie on their father, Laci would never have found her passion in surfing. So Mommy Dearest scored big brownie points in that regard. Sure, it was hard knowing her own mother didn't want her, but the fact that she hadn't much wanted her mom had made it easier. Now, Laci couldn't imagine a life without the waves and the sand, the swell and the tides. The ocean moved her.

Surfing had, in a word, saved her life. Sure, things had gotten better when she and Millie had been dumped on their dad. And he'd been awesome. But they'd never really fallen into a family routine.

On the waves, though, everything had order. She'd found a modicum of control over her own life when she was out on the waves, something she'd certainly never had with her mother, and had very little of with her dad. Surfing made sense. There was a rhythm and a predictability that came with the ocean, despite the fact that if you didn't pay her the respect she deserved, the ocean would wipe you out.

She'd found her center when she'd found surfing, and every time she stepped into the water joy crashed over her like the waves. The spray of the ocean was a calming balm, and the thrill of riding the crest of an awesome wave was nothing short of freedom.

And speak of the devil.

One beauty of a wave was coming right at her, and she was perfectly positioned. With the instinct that came from years of training, Laci popped up perfectly onto her board, her feet automatically going into position, her knees bent and her arms out for balance. All of that was part of the drill as she carved up the wave. What wasn't included in the basic surf instruction was the smile, but she couldn't help that—she was alive. A-freaking-live. And the way she skimmed along the top of the water was like flying. No, it was better. This was religion or sex or…*rapture.* Absolute, total, mind-blowing rapture.

And to think that her mother had inadvertently given her all of this.

Ironic, she thought, how sometimes the best things in your life are wrapped in pain and discontent.

Even her relationship with Taylor.

She shifted on the board, her balance suddenly unsteady. She didn't want Taylor to intrude on this moment as he had on the beach. But apparently there was no escaping him. Even out on the waves, he filled her head.

She tried to ignore her thoughts and focus on the feel of the water beneath her, but her concentration wasn't at its best right then. And instead of losing herself in the rapture, she shot a glance toward the beach, hoping to see Taylor still standing there, his eyes on her, realizing what he'd lost when he'd screwed her over.

Except he wasn't there. The bastard had left.

He'd walked away.

He'd actually done what she'd told him to.

And damn her traitorous heart, she actually cared.

LACI'S DARK MOOD was still with her when she arrived at Da Kine. She'd spent another hour on the water, but her heart hadn't been with the waves. Instead, she'd kept glancing at the beach, hoping that Taylor had simply stepped away, and that he would come back to watch her.

In her imagination, she could feel his eyes on her. The warm water triggered memories of colder Pacific shores, the chill fought off by long nights in a steamy hot tub. And it hadn't just been the water that had been steaming. Between her and Taylor, they'd generated enough heat to burn down half of Southern California.

When she'd wiped out for the second time, she realized that she needed to pack it in in case she seriously injured herself before the competition even started.

So she'd paddled to shore, trudged to the bungalow and sipped a glass of wine as she'd showered and changed. She'd hoped the wine would mellow her, but all it did was make her more melancholy. And needy.

And, dammit, itchy.

Seeing Taylor again had brought to a head how much she'd lost when she'd lost him. And damned if she didn't want to hate him for it.

More than that, though, she hated the fact that he'd made her lose control. And not just any control, but control on the waves. It was the one place that had always been hers and hers alone—the ocean.

And to Laci's way of thinking that was an unforgivable sin.

She paused on the weathered porch outside the familiar bar. Neither JC nor Drea had noticed her, their heads bent close together as they flipped pages in a catalog. Probably scoping out the latest in sex wax or skin suits.

She had every intention of stepping inside and joining them. In fact, she wanted their advice and counsel. Wanted them to kick a little sense into her, because the truth was that her anger was fading in the wake of Taylor's newest departure, and all that was left was that look she'd seen in his eyes as he'd peered down at her on the beach.

She'd seen it before; she knew what it meant. He wanted her. And so help her, despite every ounce of sanity in her body telling her to run far and fast, she wanted him, too.

Before she even realized that she'd started walking, she was off the porch and marching across the packed sand leading toward the parking area. Her feet were bare, her flip-flops dangling from her fingers, and she regretted not bringing her car. Because she wasn't going back to the bungalow. No, she had someplace else in mind.

Fifteen minutes later, she jogged up the steps to Sloane's, another local bar with a much harder-core feel. She'd been here only once before, six months before, when she'd come out on vacation with a biker buddy who'd got it in his head that he wanted to learn to surf and had recruited Laci to teach him. Since he'd bought her plane ticket and paid for her hotel room—and was a complete gentleman despite his tattooed, pierced, leathered persona—she'd been happy to come. And by the end of the week, he'd actually conquered a few waves.

He'd taken one look at Da Kine and had sworn under his breath. Two phone calls later, they'd ended up at Sloane's. Darker, with the faint scent of illegal substances in the air, the place had a Los Angeles feel, nothing like the lazy, laid-back attitude that the Aloha state was famous for.

But that was the point.

She was wired, not laid-back. And she wanted music that grated and people who didn't know her.

God forbid anyone should overhear the phone call she was about to make.

"Tequila," she said to the bartender when he came over to the seat she'd snagged at the battered bar. "Straight up."

He eyed her up and down, as if he couldn't quite figure her out. Not too surprising. Standing there in her pink shorts and pale green halter, with her flower-laden flip-flops dangling from her fingers and a tiny pink-and-yellow purse holding her money and keys, she really looked nothing like the other denizens of this place.

She smiled up at him and winked, which turned out to be great fun because the bear of a man actually reddened, his ruddy complexion turning blotchy.

She smiled again, feeling the pull of feminine power in her groin. Good. Because right then, she was all about power. She'd come here with a plan, after all. And the only way it was going to work was if she had the upper hand—and if she kept it.

Taylor Dutton had wrenched control from her and she knew what she had to do to steady herself again. She had to take it back.

With a tight smile, she dug her cell phone from her purse and called the office for the bungalows where she and the girls were staying. She doubted Taylor was there, but she had to start her search somewhere.

"I'm looking for Taylor Dutton," she said when the front desk clerk answered. "Can you connect me to his bungalow?" She'd hoped the confidence would work magic in her favor, but magic was sadly lacking, and she learned that Taylor wasn't registered there. Undaunted, she called information and got the phone numbers of the other three hotels she knew of in the area.

Nada.

She shifted in her seat, wondering if this was a sign. Yes, she wanted to prove to Taylor that he couldn't simply waltz into her life and steal her control. She wanted to surprise him—to seduce him—and then walk away leaving him gasping and frantic and wondering what the heck had just happened.

She wanted the upper hand—and she wanted it even though her head kept telling her heart that she hadn't fully thought this thing through. Because the truth was, no matter how much she firmed up her spine, where Taylor was concerned, all her good intentions might go spiraling downward in a whirlpool of lust. And that wouldn't be good. She wanted him panting for her, not the other way around.

Probably best to forget the whole thing, march out of the bar, head straight to a cold shower and do whatever utterly solo activities were required to get Taylor Dutton out of her head.

With that plan firmly in mind, she slammed back the shot of tequila, slapped down a ten-dollar bill since she was in a generous mood, and slid off the stool.

Then she turned and slammed right into something hard and lean and desperately familiar.

Taylor's chest.

She breathed in, her body tightening from the memory of his scent.

Don't go there, Laci. You'll regret it...

But she shoved the voice aside. She wanted this. No—she *needed* this.

Hadn't Taylor taken what he'd needed from her? Her skill? Her potential to help him climb through the ranks?

Hadn't he freaking used her when he'd pulled her into the San Clemente competition? Shine the media on with a little bit of sex and gossip to generate interest for an up-and-coming competition?

And now it was her turn to use him—just like she'd planned, just like she'd come here to do.

"Laci—" he began, but she cut him off, boldly grabbing him by the collar and tugging him toward her. She captured his mouth with hers, thrilled and excited by the heat that spread through her—a heat she not only wanted, but which was matched by the intensity of Taylor's reaction. A reaction that was pressing hard and thick against her thigh. And just because she could, she got closer still—any closer and she'd be wearing those khakis with him—and wriggled. Not much, but it was enough to make him groan. A low, private groan that shot through her, making her wet not only from the heat and desire arcing between them, but also from the sense of power and control. This was her moment, and she wanted to savor it.

"Outside," she whispered, her fingers knotting in his T-shirt as she tugged him toward the door. She didn't look around; it wasn't necessary. She could tell by the silence in the room that every eye was on them. And yeah, she kind of liked that, too.

"What are you doing, Laci?" he asked once she'd pushed him out the door and around the side of the building into deep shadows. "No, don't answer that. I can tell what. The question is why."

"Do you really want to know?" She watched his eyes—those decidedly male eyes—and could see his ego warring with his mind. Part of him did want to know, sure. But another part just wanted to go with it. Wanted the sex and the passion and the lust any way he could get it.

"Yeah," he said after a pause long enough to make her insides tremble. "I really want to know."

She raised her brow, and made one mental tick mark to the Taylor's-not-as-big-a-jerk-as-he-seems side of her brain. Then she shook off the inkling of respect that came with his answer; respect and Taylor simply didn't go together. Not anymore.

He was watching her face, his eyes seeing more than they should, and he stepped toward her, forcing her back against the building. "Tell me, Laci. Tell me what you're up to."

She swallowed. She could walk away now—she knew that. Walk away and leave Taylor behind and forget any of this happened. She *should*.

But she didn't.

Instead, she tilted her head up, a little smile playing at the edges of her mouth. "You thought about me, you said? Well, I thought about you, too. More than I wanted to, in fact, because I didn't want someone I hated in my head."

He winced at that, but she didn't even pause. "And this," she added, reaching down to grab his balls, "is because you screwed me over. You were the one in control, remember? And I had nothing to grab on to."

She leaned in and captured his mouth with hers. He was hot and delicious, and tasted of spice and beer and lust. She moved away from the wall to press closer against him. Her hands slid intimately over him, his erection now straining against his pants as she eased shamelessly into him, feeling its thick intensity pressed against her.

She broke the kiss and leaned toward his ear. "Right now, I'd say I'm the one with the power." And with a victorious grin, she asked, "Or would you disagree?"

4

HELL, NO, he wouldn't disagree.

Taylor didn't know exactly what Laci was up to—except for the sex, which was obvious—but his body had already made the decision that he was going to go with it.

He wasn't naive enough to think that sex with him was going to make her forget her anger and heal all their wounds and they'd ride off into the sunset for a happily ever after. But at the very least, sex was going to put them in bed together. And unless she was feeling particularly cruel, there'd be the obligatory post-coital conversation. And then a drink. And a meal.

And at some point during all of those mating rituals, he'd fall down on his knees again and beg forgiveness.

Right at the moment, though, forgiveness was the last thing on his mind. Begging, however…

Oh, yeah, she'd definitely reduced him to begging.

And before the night was over, Taylor intended to return the favor.

They'd had some of their best conversations after long nights twisting in the sheets, and he wanted her warm and pliant and seeing things his way by morning.

"Quit thinking," she whispered, her lips brushing his ear. "Quit thinking and find us a room."

"Sweetheart," he drawled, "what's the rush?" He hooked his arms around her waist and eased her closer, needing to feel all of her against him, not just her hand on his cock, no matter how good that might be. She smelled like the ocean, and he imagined her taking the quickest of showers after coming in off the beach, then slipping into the delicious barely there outfit that he desperately wanted off her.

As if to prove the point, he kept one hand on her bare back and moved the other to her breast. Her pert nipple pressed against the palm of his hand, the thin cotton of her halter doing little more than providing basic modesty. In one flick of a finger, he thrust it aside and slid his hand inside. Her breast fitted perfectly in his palm, and he closed his eyes, fighting the urge to bend down and bring his mouth to her breast. His cock twitched in his pants, ready for action, and every molecule in his body seemed to hum with the memory of her flesh, her scent.

Dear God, he thought. *He'd missed her.*

"Hold up there, ace," she said, stepping back. "This isn't your party."

"No? 'Cause, sweetheart, it feels like my birthday and Christmas all rolled into one."

He thought he saw the firm, thin line of her mouth twitch in amusement, but in the dark, it was hard to be sure.

"No way," she said, her voice sensual yet firm. "I told you you're not calling the shots here, bud." She closed her fingers around the waistband of his slacks, then tugged him close. He came without hesitation, aroused, excited and curious to see exactly where she was taking this.

She leaned in so that he could see her face clearly in the dim light. She smiled, her mouth curving up with possessiveness and purpose. "Kiss me," she demanded.

He didn't hesitate, his body firing as her mouth opened hungrily under his, hot and demanding and oh so insistent. She tasted like the ocean laced with sunshine, and he wanted to drown in her. To sink into her depths and never rise again.

Poetic, sappy and probably stupid, but he couldn't help the way he felt. The way she made him feel.

"No," she murmured as he tried to snake his hands down to her ass. She broke their kiss only for the single, whispered word, then slid back into him, devouring, tasting and consuming.

She was making him crazy, and he wanted to touch, to

explore, to *feel*. What he didn't want was to break her rules. Because he knew damn well what the punishment would be.

She'd leave.

And who the hell knew if she'd come back.

Not that this was exactly punishment, he had to admit, as her tongue danced and teased inside his mouth and her clever fingers slid down under the waistband of his pants. Torture, maybe, but definitely not punishment.

"Do you like that?" she whispered, sliding her lips over his cheek to nibble on his earlobe. "How about this?" she asked, making him groan as her palm closed around his cock, fully erect and desperate to be free. "Yeah," she said. "I think you do."

"Laci…" That was all he could manage. All the communication that his addled brain could handle.

"Shhh," she said, slowly stroking him, her hand gliding over the length of him, her hand so soft and firm. So sweet, so perfect.

"Should I make you come?" she asked, with such wide-eyed innocence that it was a wonder he didn't come right then. "No," she answered herself, and he stifled a groan, his body screaming for a release that she wasn't yet ready to give. "Good choice. Not yet. Let's make this last a little longer."

"Laci, please," he managed, his voice ragged.

"No, no. No 'please.' Just thank you. Say 'thank you,' Taylor."

He met her eyes, saw the delight dancing there. She knew what she was doing to him, and she was reveling in it.

And instead of irritating him, that tiny fact turned him on that much more.

Damned if he wasn't a goner. A frustrated, blue-balled, hopelessly-in-lust goner.

"Say it," she insisted, giving his balls a quick squeeze, as if she'd just read his mind.

"Thank you, Laci," he replied, and watched the smile bloom across her face.

"Aren't you polite? Well, then," she said, leaning in confidentially. "In that case maybe I'll give you an extra treat."

She stroked him one long, last time, and he shuddered as her hand moved over his tight flesh. Then she slipped her hand out of his pants, leaving his skin aching for the warmth of her touch, and his mind humming with unfulfilled lust. "What…?" he managed, and even that took all of his mental effort.

She reached into his pockets and plucked out his keys. "Parking lot?"

He nodded. "Blue cargo van." He'd wanted to rent a convertible, but he'd gotten stuck with one of XtremeSportNet's vehicles. A fact that had initially irritated him; now, it seemed like kismet. Convertibles might have a reputation for getting a woman hot, but that wasn't an issue at the moment. Privacy, however, was. And the windowless van had privacy in spades.

"I would have pegged you as a Jaguar type," she said once they reached the lot and stood in front of the van.

"Hell, no. A Mustang." He grinned. "We Southern boys don't cotton to them big-city cars," he added, laying the accent on thick.

She laughed—a real laugh, not out of politeness or nervousness and certainly not part of this little sexcapade she had going for his benefit. Or her benefit. To be honest, he wasn't sure about that. All he knew was that he was enjoying himself. He had an X and a Y chromosome after all.

He took a step toward the driver's-side door, but she tugged him back, her hand tight in his. "Not necessary," she said. "We're not going anywhere."

While he gaped, she opened the back of the van, then grunted appreciatively when she saw the carpeted rear compartment. In the morning, it would be filled with surfboards. Right now, it had nothing more than some board wax, a few towels and six boxes of XtremeSportNet flyers advertising Girls Go Banzai. Tomorrow, a crew of eager young college kids would blanket the area with the flyers.

Tonight, Taylor was grateful for the carpeting. He lifted his foot up to the back bumper, then reached out a hand for her. Her expression shifted, and he could almost see the debate going on in her head. She'd started this, after all, but now he was taking control, inviting her into his domain. Her idea, yeah. But it was his hand extended in invitation.

A whisper of something washed over his face, and though she said nothing, he could almost hear her philosophical *What the hell?* as she grabbed his hand and allowed him to haul her up.

That, however, was where he lost the momentum. Because as soon as she had both feet on the deck and her balance restored, she planted her hands on his shoulders and pressed him back on that automotive carpet, and Laci was straddling him. "Laci—" he began, but she silenced him with a finger to his lips, then followed that with a fingertip to his neck, down to his chest, his crotch.

"Too many clothes," she whispered, her fingers going to work on the button on his khakis, then easing the zipper down as he winced, too aroused and too sane not to fear physical damage to highly valued parts of his body.

"Ah, um, careful there."

"Don't worry. Right now, I'm as much invested in that bit of anatomy as you are." She grinned up at him, all lust and easy control. "I promise I'll be gentle."

She eased his pants down over his hips, her grin widening when his cock sprang to attention. "Nice to see I still have that effect on you," she said, and though he could hear the matter-of-fact tone in her voice, he told himself there was something more. A hint of regret, a dab of real attraction over and above this power play she had going.

Because that was what this was. He knew it. Was absolutely certain.

She wasn't interested in him or in sex or in forging any sort of connection between them. Right now, all Laci wanted was control. She wanted to use him. And damned if right then, Taylor didn't want to be used.

Her hands traced up his chest, her soft fingers nimble and demanding, and the feeling was so very, very sweet. He reached down to the silky thickness of her hair, then shivered when her hot breath hit him at the pubic bone. "No, no, no," she said, taking her hands off his chest long enough to remove his fingers from her hair. "No touching, ace."

"Brutal," he whispered, grinning.

That smile lasted only a second, though, as his face shifted to startled ecstasy when her mouth slipped over his cock. Her tongue teased him, nudging him closer and closer to a place he wanted to go—did he ever—but desperately didn't want to go alone.

"Laci—" Her name slipped from his lips, his voice harsh and hot and almost unrecognizable to his own ears. And though he knew she wanted to be in control, he couldn't take it. He had to be inside her. Had to feel her quiver and tighten like a velvet fist around him.

He could still remember the low moans and soft stutter of breath when she came, and he needed to hear them now. Needed to hear them for him.

"*Laci.*" There was control in his words this time. His control, and he pulled her off him, shivering at the sensation of his mouth-warmed cock sliding out into the cool night air.

"You want me, sport?"

"Hell, yes," he groaned.

"Good." The smile she flashed him was pure feminine power. "Do you remember the rules? No touching. Touch," she repeated, "and it's all over."

He nodded, compliant as a puppy, though he secretly doubted that she'd stop if he touched her. Not if he waited until she was far enough along, anyway.

But he was a man who knew how to follow the rules. She wanted his hands off her? He could do that. He could do it because he firmly believed that next time, his hands would be all over her.

While he watched, the woman straddling him from his prone position, she wriggled out of her shorts. He groaned at the sight of her, naked and beautiful over him, her tanned skin glowing in the dim light of the van.

Above them, he heard the faint *ping, ping* of raindrops starting to fall, and he bit back a curse. Yeah, the storms the weathermen had predicted would wreak havoc with XtremeSportNet's competition prep, but that wasn't his problem. As far as he knew, it was dry as a bone in Sydney, and the only wetness that mattered to him was the sweet dew between Laci's legs.

She met his eyes, her expression bland except for the amusement glowing in her eyes. "Eager?"

"Absolutely," he said, with absolutely no shame.

A genuine smile touched her lips. "Me, too," she said, then eased forward. She dug a condom out of her tiny purse and grinned impishly as she rolled it over him, that touch alone almost enough to make him come. But there was more, so much more sweet torture, and when he was properly sheathed, she lifted her hips, rose over him and impaled herself on him. She arched her back, a breathy moan escaping as her mouth opened and her eyes closed.

Ecstasy, he thought, and said a silent thank-you that he'd been the man she'd shared it with.

She started to move then, and all thoughts evaporated from his brain, replaced with only the delirious sensation of moving toward something huge and explosive. His eyes closed, and he breathed in deeply, wanting simply to feel, to experience. More than that, though, he wanted to watch, and so he peeled his eyes open and used the few coherent brain cells he had left to enjoy watching Laci writhe on top of him.

At first, she looked powerful, in control. But as he watched—as his own climax came barreling toward him and her body squeezed and shuddered against him—her expression changed, softened. She was in control, yes, but she was also lost in the moment. Enjoying herself. Enjoying *him.*

He hoped so. Truly.

He knew the moment she came, her muscles tightening around him, sending him over the edge only seconds behind her.

"There is a heaven," he muttered, and her short, soft laugh in response delighted him.

He broke the rules then, by reaching up and stroking her cheek. Then he gently eased her down, holding his breath as she stiffened before loosening up again and sliding gracefully into the crook of his arm.

"Are we done?" he asked, careful to keep a tease in his voice despite his fear that the answer was yes, and that she'd pull on her clothes and skip out of the van without once looking back.

"Done? I'm wiped." She edged up on her elbow, raised an eyebrow, the innocent-looking freckles that dotted her nose destroying the image of the in-control vixen she'd just played out on his cock. "Why? Is there something more you want?"

She tossed the words out casually, but he thought he heard a real question in there. Maybe even hope.

Or maybe he was engaging in some serious wishful thinking.

He considered shaking his head and keeping silent, but he wasn't a man to run away from things that scared him. And the one time in his life he'd failed to chase down something he'd wanted, it had slipped through his fingers. *She* had slipped through his fingers.

He wasn't going to let that happen again.

"You," he said, putting every scrap of sincerity he could muster into his voice. It wasn't hard because he was as sincere as they came. And from the shocked expression on her face, he had a feeling she knew that.

"You sure about that?" she asked lightly.

"I want you, Laci," he repeated. "I've always wanted you."

Her brow furrowed and she scooted away from him, searching the interior of the van until she found a crumpled beach towel. She dragged it toward her and slipped it over her shoulders, letting it hang down, covering all of her.

He bit back a sigh, understanding she felt exposed, but not willing to back down because this was too important. *Laci* was too important. "I'm sorry," he said, then paused to let the words hang between them before continuing. "I'm sitting here in the back of a rented van, half-naked, and I'm telling you that I'm sorry."

She opened her mouth to speak, didn't manage it, and closed it again. But he saw questions in her eyes. Questions and a hurt he wanted to help heal.

He reached out and broke the rules again, this time by cupping her face. "I never meant to hurt you."

"But you did," she said, her voice soft. Timid.

"I know." He still didn't completely understand the why of it, but all that mattered right now was his regret and their probably futile attempt to somehow make it all better.

"I'm sorry," he said, meaning it fully. "I am honestly and truly sorry that I hurt you."

SHE WAS an idiot.

She knew she was an idiot because she believed him. He said he was sorry in that Southern Comfort voice, and she looked into those eyes and damned if she didn't believe that every word he said was true.

She didn't know if she was a fool or if he was a lying jerk or if it was a combination of both.

Or maybe—just maybe—Fate was giving them a second chance.

Because no matter how much he'd hurt her in the past, the band around her chest was dissolving. His presence alone had begun to strip it from her, and when he'd smiled, standing over her on the beach, the desire so clear in his eyes, that had loosened the band, as well.

But it was here, in the dark, in the back of this absurd van that she *knew*. This wasn't about her being in control or him getting off on her Hot-Girl-in-the-City routine. This was Taylor doing penance. This was Taylor genuinely sorry. This was Taylor apologizing.

Most important, this was Taylor wanting her, just like he said.

He was watching her now with hooded, worried eyes. "I can say I'm sorry again if you want," he whispered. "I'll say it as many times as I need to."

She licked her lips, wanting to trust him, but not wanting to be stupid. And sure as hell not wanting to get burned again. "Why are you here?"

He flashed that quick grin that had made her fall for him, and she forced herself to stay strong this time. "Because you didn't want to go back to my place."

It was her turn to grin. "On the island, Taylor. Why are you on this island?"

"Because of you," he said without hesitation.

"Me?"

He drew in a breath, as if what he had to say was important, and he knew it. "I'm here because I wanted to see you again. I'm here to make this right between us."

"No bullshit?"

"No bullshit."

She *was* an idiot. And she was about to do something really stupid.

She was about to hold out her hand to him and ask him to take her to bed.

And all she could do beyond that was hope and pray that she wasn't making the second-biggest mistake of her life.

5

Two HOURS later, her bare legs wrapped in cool sheets and a naked man standing across the room pouring her a glass of sparkling water, Laci had to admit that if this was a mistake, at least she was going out with a bang.

Three bangs, actually, at last count, and she felt positively, wonderfully boneless.

"You look content," he said, coming back to her with the water.

She smiled, boldly watching him move, enjoying the easy way they were together, just like they'd been before San Clemente. "I am," she said, refusing to let her memories destroy her mood. "I think you've melted my insides."

"Good for me," he said, then sat down beside her on the edge of the bed. Her hand drifted to his knee, and she let her fingers idly glide over his thigh, the perfect intimacy of it delighting her. Hard to believe it was true, but in these few short hours they'd fallen back into their routine. A routine that had once comforted and excited her.

A routine that had had her thoughts turning to marriage and family and permanence.

A routine that had been ripped away from her when he'd screwed her over for his career.

"Uh-oh," he said, looking at her face. "What did I do?"

She shook her head, determined not to be the kind of person who clung to bitterness. He'd come to her on his knees, wanting forgiveness, and she'd granted it. She wasn't going to destroy what they now had growing between them by dwelling on the past. "Absolutely nothing," she assured him. "At least nothing bad."

"Then why the frown?"

She curved her mouth into a smile. "Maybe I'm thinking about tomorrow and the next day. Maybe I'm thinking that I don't want to leave here."

"Then don't." He took her hand. "Stay."

She laughed. "My roommates would get worried."

"Just for the weekend. I have to leave for Sydney early next week."

A hard knot of disappointment settled in her stomach. "I'll miss you," she admitted, taking the plunge, and gratified by the way his eyes lit up.

"It doesn't have to be goodbye," he said. "More like a see you later. You finish here, you can come down there. I could still get you in the competition if you want. Or—" he added quickly, apparently seeing the look on her face "—you can just hang with me." He took her hand, looked into her eyes. "This isn't about your surfboard, Laci. It's about you. About us. I missed you. God, I missed you something fierce."

"I missed you, too," she admitted, then leaned against him with a sigh. "I guess I could stay here for a few days." She glanced toward the sliding-glass door onto his balcony. He was staying at one of the high-rise hotels just off the beach, and the storm was blasting away at the glass. The weathermen had predicted violent winds, most blasting inland, which would destroy any chance of decent surfing even during lulls in the deluge.

Or possibly she was simply looking for excuses to stay inside, dry and warm, with Taylor.

What the hell. She slid her legs over the side of the bed and padded to the dresser where she'd left her cell phone, the weight of Taylor's eyes following her the entire way. Since she wasn't in the mood to answer questions, she didn't call either JC or Drea directly. Instead, she called the main number at the inn and left a message, telling the desk clerk to relay to her friends that Laci had run across an old friend, and they were going to spend the weekend catching up.

"Have fun," the front-desk clerk said, and Laci rolled her eyes.

The clerk was about eighteen, and more than capable of reading between the lines. Who knew what she'd tell JC and Drea.

Laci decided she didn't care. Considering what she intended to do with the man for the next two days, whatever the clerk opined probably wouldn't even come close to reality.

APPARENTLY, taking his vitamins, saying his prayers and being nice to puppies had paid off, Taylor thought, because there could be no doubt at all that his prayers had been answered, his dreams had come true and every other corny clichéd line about wish-fulfillment that he could think of had manifested right there with Laci.

She wasn't going anywhere.

He knew that because they'd already spent the night together and now it was lunchtime on Saturday, and they were still going strong. And no, not just sexually, though the last time he'd had so much fun in bed had been fourteen months ago with this very woman.

No, they were going strong together. Connecting. Talking and laughing and generally hanging out.

And yeah, a tiny part of him wanted to believe they were falling in love all over again, but he wasn't quite willing to believe that yet, no matter how much he might want to.

They'd talked about nothing and everything, carefully avoiding the past as if they both knew that they simply needed to get beyond it in order to heal. He'd told her about Georgia and how his father had struggled as a carpenter while the family had lived in a small shack on the grounds of a big house in Atlanta where his mother worked as the cook. He still remembered the day that all the fancy cars had arrived at the house for some big-deal party. He'd gone in the back door to ask his mother something, and the owner of the house had caught him, said things that made it clear that he wasn't welcome inside. Not then. Not when the money was there.

"And so you decided then and there to make your own money?" she asked. She was naked, on her stomach, draped across the bed. Her feet were up and crossed, and her chin rested on her fists. She looked, he thought, about as sexy as he'd ever seen her.

"I know it sounds like a soap-opera plot, but it's true. Money, and the respect that goes with it. How about you?"

"And you're doing well," she said, dodging his question. "XtremeSportNet's a great outfit. How long have you been with them?"

"About a year," he said, leaving unspoken the fact that Reggie had hired him fresh off San Clemente. "And yeah. It's a good gig. Reggie's a hard taskmaster, but he's a good trainer, and he promotes up through the ranks."

Her smile was genuine. "I'm happy for you."

"How's Millie enjoying stardom? She stole the show when I saw it."

"What?" Laci asked, sitting up and pulling a sheet up to cover her. Taylor laughed, completely enjoying how flabbergasted his comment had made her.

"I'm working in Sydney right now, remember? I went and saw *The Magic Flute* a few weeks ago when I was in town to lock down some vendors and locations."

"You're an opera fan?" she asked, and he had to laugh at the utter disbelief on her face. Well, why not? He *wasn't* an opera fan, and she knew him well enough to know that.

"I'm not," he said, then met her eyes. "But she's your sister."

Laci's hand went to her mouth. "Taylor," she whispered, her eyes welling with tears.

"Don't cry," he said, pulling her close. "It wasn't torture. The opera was really good."

That made Laci laugh, and the sound delighted him. He liked her laugh, liked her happy. And right then he felt the sappy, overwhelming desire to make her happy for the rest of her life.

"I missed you," he said softly, using the pad of his thumb to wipe away her tear.

"I missed you, too," she said, turning so that the sheet was the only thing between them. She sighed softly and hooked her arms around his neck. "Thanks for coming here for me. I'm sorry we waited so long. So many months. I feel like we need to make up for lost time."

"You're welcome," he said, nipping at her bottom lip. "And I think that we definitely have some catching up to do."

He pressed his mouth to hers, his body firing with desire as she melted against him, no longer with retribution or a need for control, but now with a woman's need to be with a man. It humbled him to realize that he was that man. Humbled him, and turned him on. Powerfully and desperately.

He leaned back, putting an inch of distance between them, and feeling the smooth glide of the silk sheet as it slid over her breasts to pool over their hips and thighs. He dipped his head, his tongue laving her nipple, his heart beating wildly with an overpowering lust coupled with a tender longing that came close to driving him mad. "Let me take care of you," he whispered. "Let me make you come."

LET ME make you come.

He'd dropped that little suggestion on her Saturday, and now, late on Sunday, she had to say he'd certainly kept up his end of the bargain. She'd had so many orgasms her body was in a state of nonstop tingling, and they'd taken so many showers together it was amazing they both weren't prunes.

They'd ordered in exclusively, and had spent the entire weekend talking or making love.

The truth was, she'd enjoyed both activities equally. She'd always enjoyed Taylor's company; he was the only man she'd ever been able to talk openly with, to feel genuinely comfortable around. He'd been more than a lover, he'd been her best friend, and now that she was back in his arms, she could admit to herself how much she'd lost when she'd walked away from him—when what he'd done had forced her away.

Don't go there, Laci, she warned herself. *Fresh starts, remember?*

Now, she stood in the shower alone as Taylor lounged on the bed, drinking wine and channel-surfing. She tilted her face up for the spray of water and smiled. So like a guy.

And since he was so entrenched with ESPN, she was genuinely surprised when warm hands cupped her naked breasts, and the insistent press of a fully aroused penis thrust against the curve of her butt.

"Oh, Michael," she said, remembering the name of the room-service waiter. "You shouldn't have come now. My boyfriend's in the other room."

"Your boyfriend's a lucky man," he said, sliding soapy hands down her belly, his clever fingers finding her cleft even as his cock pressed hard against her ass. His mouth nipped at her ear as one hand traveled up to stroke her breast, the other finding and teasing her clit. "Do you mean that?" he whispered. "Boyfriend?"

She could barely breathe for the havoc he was wreaking on her, but she managed a soft, breathy "yes."

"Sweetheart," he murmured, the passion evident in both his voice and his clever hands moving over her skin. Her body was so primed from having been so deliciously loved for days that she came right then, shuddering and breaking into a million glowing pieces. He stroked her and held her, his fingertips dancing all over her skin, his warm heat helping to put her back together again.

"That was nice," he said, reaching behind her to turn off the water. "But I think we need the bed to finish it properly."

She felt half-melted, so sated she could barely even giggle when he picked her up bride-style and carried her to the bed. He straddled her, his hands and mouth working over every inch of her. She was already ready, of course, but damned if he didn't make her more so. Damned if he didn't make her beg.

And when she did, he didn't tease. His gentle hands cupped her thighs, pushing her legs apart. And then, with one strong thrust, he entered her, then slid in and out rhythmically, gaining power with each thrust, as she lifted her hips to meet him, to bring him deeper.

Finally, when she was certain she could take it no longer, he came, and she joined him, clinging and gasping, until they were both spent and exhausted, collapsed in a tangle on the sweat-soaked sheets.

After an eternity, she stretched against him, the glow of great sex still clinging to her like bath oil, warm and slippery and deliciously comforting. "You really have to go away?"

"I could quit my job," he said. "We could live here in this hotel room forever."

"I like it," she said.

"So do I." He propped himself up on his elbows and started to stroke his fingers up and down her bare back. The sensation was delicious and for a brief moment she considered twisting around and using her own hands and lips to draw him back down into the sweet abyss of sex. She fought the urge, though, and instead twisted around to smile at him.

"I'm glad you made the trip," she said. "It's nice to know you came just for me. That you're not doing anything with Banzai."

A shadow crossed his eyes, and her heart twisted, afraid despite the days they'd just shared that she'd judged him wrongly. But no. That wasn't possible.

Still, though, she had to ask. "What?"

"Actually, that's not true. About Banzai."

Her heart tightened, and she feared the worst. Some confession, now drawn out of him from guilt, perhaps. Something horrible, since anything that made her want to back away from him again *would* be horrible.

The realization hit her with a jolt. She actually shifted a little on the bed, disturbed by how quickly she'd gone from wanting to burn him in effigy to wanting him back in her life. Needing him back in her life.

Except the truth was, she'd never truly wanted him to burn. She'd wanted back the man she'd fallen in love with—because she *had* been desperately, hopelessly, painfully in love—but she'd been so angry about the way he'd hurt her that her wish had seemed impossible, their troubles insurmountable.

But now here he was, apologizing and wanting her and being the man she'd yearned for.

And also scaring her with that shadow in his eye that suggested lies and fears and the return to a bitterness between them that, so help her, she wanted to forget.

Bottom line? She wanted him back. And the thought that he was now about to blow it between them terrified her.

She swallowed, then met his eyes. "Tell me," she demanded.

"I told Reggie I'd pass out those fliers. The ones in the van," he clarified. "Apparently, Morgan didn't bother to put the word out to the local kids and he doesn't have enough manpower. So technically I've been demoted."

Relief—then laughter—bubbled through her. "You bastard! You knew I'd be thinking all sorts of terrible things," she said, and was struck by how big a step that was. That they could joke now about the bad history they'd finally put behind them.

"Hey," he said defensively. "Handing out fliers *is* terrible."

"I could help," she said. He cocked his head, looking at her, and suddenly she felt foolish. "I mean, if you want me to."

The grin that spread over his face erased all her fears. "I'd love it, but wouldn't you rather be beating the waves than the pavement?" He nodded toward the sliding-glass door, beyond which the afternoon sun shone clear and bright.

She shrugged, then reached for his hand. "I'd rather be with you."

His brows rode up, challenging, and she laughed, warm and delighted. It had always been so easy to laugh with him.

"Okay, fair enough," she amended. "I am getting homesick for the waves. But that doesn't mean I don't want you, too." She stroked her finger on his cheek, enjoying the freedom to touch him intimately. "I'll have to lose myself in practice. Make sure I win so that you'll come rushing back to congratulate me."

"I've seen you surf," he said. "And I'm certain you'll win. And when you do, I'll be right beside you."

For a second, the past intruded, San Clemente welling up all around her, along with the humiliation that came with the knowledge that he'd brought her in as a wild card because he was sleeping with her, not because of her talent.

But that was then, she told herself. This weekend had been about moving on.

But once again, she hoped she was thinking with her head and not with her hormones. Because hormones had a way of really messing a girl up.

"Second thoughts?" he asked, his narrowed eyes searching her face. His tone was light, but she could see the worry, and it was that more than anything that had her shaking her head in the negative.

"None," she said, drawing strength from certainty. "Absolutely none."

LONG SHADOWS fell across the beach by the time they came up for air again. Figuratively, of course, since they'd been swimming in an ocean of sex on a sea of silk sheets and wine.

"Now I'm thinking screw the contest," Laci said. "I don't have a choice since I'm going to be here, with you, two weeks from now."

"They'll find our shriveled corpses," Taylor concurred. "Starved, but not for sex."

"Sated," she said. "Dead, sated and happy."

"We could order room service," he suggested, and her stomach gurgled in response. "And that answered that question," he added with a laugh.

He slid off the bed, naked, and crossed the room. "Something different this time? Maybe—" he began, but was cut off by the ringing of the phone. "Maybe they heard us and the food cart's on the way. Hello?" he edged the handset between his chin and shoulder and started flipping through the menu. "What?"

Laci sat up. She could tell by the invisible rod that suddenly straightened his posture that work had intruded on their fantasy. She started running through scenarios in her head, telling herself that this party had to come to an end sooner or later, and she could be a big girl and not whine when he had to cut their date short. Not that it had been all that short, but still…

"I'm sorry," he said when he hung up. "I have to swing by the office."

"It's the middle of the night."

"Reggie never sleeps."

"I'm being completely selfish, but I don't want you to go."

"I'm being completely selfish and admitting that I like to hear that." He came over to her and kissed the tip of her nose. "But I still have to go."

"I know." She glanced at the clock, and asked, "Should I wait?"

He shook his head, and her insides tensed, feeling foolish and afraid suddenly that she'd gotten this all wrong. "Go on back to your bungalow," he said. "This may be an all-nighter."

"Okay," she said, and told herself silently that he was being perfectly reasonable. This wasn't a brush-off. This was basic human interaction.

"About tomorrow," he began.

"Yes?"

"I thought maybe I could take you to brunch. A real meal. A date, even." He swept his arm around the sex-ravaged room. "This was fabulous, but I thought maybe we could try for a bit more romance. I know a great place with champagne and lobster and a fabulous view. Would that be okay?"

She knew he could guess her answer because there was no way she could keep the smile off her face. Since, yeah, she was really starting to believe her own fantasy. Really starting to believe that they could pick up where they had left off and erase all the bad stuff. That this interlude in a hotel suite was more than just a sexual diversion. She beamed up at him, delighted to find him beaming right back. "Yes," she said. "I'd love to go out on a date with you."

6

LACI DIDN'T surf the next morning, but she did get up with the sun and go out to the beach. Neither Drea nor JC were up when she rose, and for that, she was grateful. They'd been asleep when she'd come home the night before, and she'd been grateful for that, too. No matter how much she loved her friends, she hadn't wanted to talk about what had happened with Taylor.

Instead, she'd wanted to savor.

She'd fallen into her bed without showering, wanting the scent of Taylor around her as she slept so that the essence of him would fill her dreams.

It had worked, too. Sweet dreams were nothing compared to the sensual, erotic places her mind took her. Or where Taylor took her in her mind.

She'd awakened giddy, and when she'd looked at herself in the mirror she almost didn't recognize her face, so wide was her smile.

"Hopeless," she'd whispered to her reflection. She'd slipped on shorts and a T-shirt, not bothered with shoes, and padded through the living room to the door. She'd left the quiet house behind and moved to the surf, the pull and tug of the waves against the sand reminding her of Taylor's sweet, rhythmic thrusts.

Oh, yes, she had it bad. And it was even kind of nice to admit it.

She walked in the surf for another few hours before heading back to the bungalow. The lights were on and she heard the hum of music and could see JC and Drea moving around inside. As soon as she pulled open the weather-beaten screen door, she saw Drea perched at the breakfast counter and JC in the kitchen scowling at a cup of coffee. Both of them turned to her as she entered, their faces grave.

"What?" Reflexively, Laci looked behind her. "What's going on?"

They exchanged a look. The kind of look that friends used when they had news to share that they absolutely did not want to reveal. The kind of look that made Laci nervous. "What?" she repeated. "Out with it. Whatever it is can't be that bad. I'm in too good a mood this morning and I absolutely refuse to let anything muck it up."

Another silent communication passed between her friends, and then Drea lifted her shoulder ever so slightly. JC drew in a breath. And Laci got very, very nervous.

"Guys?"

"It is him," JC blurted out. "Taylor Dutton. He *is* here."

The fear that had threatened to suck the air out of Laci's lungs vanished in a puff, and she laughed. "I know," she said, aiming for the refrigerator. "But you guys are totally sweet to worry."

"You know?" The exchanged looks, and then the realization hit them both at the same time.

"Oh, my—" Drea said. "He was the reason for the message."

"You've been with Taylor?" JC asked. "Laci! What were you thinking?"

She could feel her cheeks heat. "We, um, sort of bumped into each other."

"And?" There was an urgency to Drea's voice that made Laci hesitate.

"We, um, had a really nice time," she said blandly.

"A nice time? With Taylor? The man you've been planning to burn in effigy for the last year?"

Okay, obviously this was the source of the weirdness. Her friends were worried about her, and rightfully so. "I'm over it," she announced, then held up a hand at their amazed faces. "No, seriously. He was utterly and totally contrite. He hates what he did to me back in California—it's been eating him up inside, too, and he came here instead of going straight to Sydney for the Danger competition because he knew I was here. He wanted to make up, guys. And we did. And," she added, although she knew her cheeks were on fire, "it was really, really nice."

Warm now, both from embarrassment and the mental playback of just how "nice" it had been, she moved into the kitchen and poured a tall glass of OJ. She took a long sip and watched her friends. JC and Drea were still staring, but now they were fidgeting, too. "Honestly, you guys? What?"

"It's just that he hurt you, Laci. Bad. Is he really the kind of guy you want to get back together with?" JC drummed her fingers on the counter and examined Laci with wide, serious eyes.

"What if he's shining you on?" Drea asked. "I mean, I don't want to say that he *is,* but don't you think you should be careful?" She glanced over at JC as if for support. "I mean, now's not the time you want to get off your game, right?"

Laci knew Drea had a point, but it wasn't one she wanted to acknowledge. Not after last night. Not after she'd stared in Taylor's eyes and seen both remorse and desire.

He was genuinely sorry he'd hurt her; she'd seen that. Understood it.

And if she knew one thing above all else, it was that he wasn't going to hurt her again.

She *had* to believe that if she wanted to make a go of a renewed relationship with Taylor. She had to start from a position of trust.

Because if she couldn't trust him, then the last forty-eight hours were nothing but smoke and mirrors.

If she couldn't trust him, she was still all alone.

TAYLOR'S MEETING with Reggie had ended some time ago, but his head was still spinning from all that had happened. Morgan getting the ax from Reggie for "extreme nonperformance," and Taylor getting pushed into Morgan's now-empty shoes without ceremony, yet with a hell of a lot of expectations.

Big expectations. Because Reggie had done a lot of blowing smoke up Taylor's ass telling him what a comer he was, and how Taylor had the mojo to get the promo and money opps going for

Banzai even as he continued to organize the Danger Down Under Competition in Sydney.

A huge responsibility with pretty much his entire career riding on it.

Honestly, Taylor wasn't certain why Reggie hadn't brought someone else in to take over from Morgan, especially since Taylor was already committed to the gills. But he hadn't. He'd tagged Taylor, and Taylor fully intended to step up to the plate.

Prove he could do this, and he'd be in solid with Reggie and XtremeSportNet, the corporate ladder his for the climbing and his Christmas bonus big enough to make his head do a solid Linda Blair number.

And that wasn't all, Taylor thought as he blindly paced his hotel room. Reggie'd also assigned the responsibility for a pre-Banzai exhibition on him. A last-minute, balls-to-the-wall demonstration of the mad skills the competition's featured surfers were going to be displaying when they rode the pipe. Not *on* the pipe, of course—for that, folks would have to wait for the day of competition. But whetting their appetite…

Oh, yeah. Taylor had to say that it was brilliant. Definitely a marketing move worthy of Reggie Pierce. The man had started out in promotions just like Taylor and made a fortune. There was no one better Taylor could learn from, and to have been hand-picked to take over these three key projects was a vote of confidence that had Taylor's head swelling to Goodyear-blimp proportions.

He frowned, realizing that he wasn't the only one this could be good for. The fact that Laci was raised in Australia meant that he could do an entire promo campaign around her, possibly even pulling in some serious endorsement dollars. She hadn't said as much, but he knew she could use the influx of cash. So far, her star was climbing, but as of yet, her pocketbook hadn't followed suit.

The Danger slate wasn't so solid that he couldn't tweak it a bit. He could bring her in as a headliner in the exhibition and she'd soon be soaring high, especially since he intended to orchestrate a dual-country pre-Banzai exhibition, with footage piped in from Australia contemporaneously with the Hawaiian event. A media spectacle, and if he could pull it off, it would make his career.

It could make Laci's, too, if only she'd let it.

He frowned, fearing he already knew how that suggestion would fly. After all, that very thing was what had ripped her from him previously.

Then, however, he hadn't talked to her beforehand.

Now they were on an even keel again, and that meant the world to him. So he wasn't about to do a damn thing without her okay. Not even if Reggie ordered him to. Some things, he thought, were more important than career advancement, and Laci Montgomery was one of those things.

He'd blown it once.

He wasn't going to blow it again.

"I'M GLAD you called," Laci said. "I was afraid that you'd had to jet off to Sydney. Or that Reggie was keeping you chained up working."

"If I'd had to leave, I would have told you," Taylor assured her. "And if it was only chains, I could break them." He stopped walking long enough to pull a muscle-man pose. She laughed and squeezed his biceps, oohing and aahing appropriately. And, she realized, having a wonderful time merely hanging out with him, doing nothing more interesting than walking hand in hand down the beach.

Of course, the beach did happen to be in Hawaii, and that definitely upped the romance factor. Add in the fact that it was now sunset and the sky screamed with color so vivid she imagined she could breathe in the night, and there was no escaping the fact that romance was in the air.

Then again, the way she was feeling about Taylor lately, they could be walking down a grubby alley and she'd still be tumbling hopelessly, madly in love.

She stumbled, the word in her head reaching down to make her trip over her own feet.

"Okay?" he said, looking sideways at her.

"Sure. Yeah. Fine."

Love.

Had she really thought that? Had she come full circle back to loving this man?

More importantly, had she ever stopped loving him?

As if he knew she was thinking of him, his fingers tightened against her own, and she drew in a shaky breath, that single, simple contact making her feel light and giddy.

Yeah, the love was still there, and the thought that they now had a chance to make it grow made her feel lighter than air. She could only hope that he felt the same way. And now, as night fell soft around them, she was determined to find out.

She tugged him to a stop. "Hey," she said. "Nice sunset."

"I ordered it especially for you."

She grinned, then tilted her head up for a quick kiss. "So I thought we should talk…"

"Sure. I have some stuff I want to talk to you about, too."

She caught his expression, the hint of seriousness under the light tone of his voice. "You first."

For a moment, he looked as if he might argue, then he nodded. Then he paused again. "To be honest, I'm not entirely sure where to start."

She frowned, some hesitancy in his voice making her suddenly uncomfortable. Although she wanted to squeeze his hand and tell him he could talk to her about anything, she found herself shoving both hands into her pockets, her eyes on her toes in the sand rather than on him. "Maybe you should just start at the beginning," she said, and her tone was so morose that he scrutinized her, and then laughed. She stood up straighter, on the defensive. "What?"

He brushed her hair out of her face. "Just because I don't know where to begin doesn't mean it's bad," he reassured.

She rolled her eyes, feeling foolish for being caught out. "Sorry. I—"

"Taylor!" A man's voice interrupted her, and she turned to see a warrior of a man in a business suit striding toward them, his pants legs rolled up and his jacket slung over his shoulder. It was an odd beach look, but it actually suited him.

"Reggie," Taylor blurted, coming to a stop and waiting for his boss to catch up with him.

"Glad I found you," Reggie said. "I've got cocktails in an hour for some potential sponsors. I couldn't get you on your cell, but I want you there. The concierge thought I might find you here."

"Scouting locations," Taylor explained, as Laci wondered what the locations could possibly be for. "Sorry about the cell. Service is spotty around here."

"I've noticed." He turned and smiled at Laci, and she could see exactly how he'd become so ferociously rich. There was a boldness in his eyes. A take-no-prisoners attitude. He was a man people would either like or hate. She doubted there was any middle ground, and just then she didn't know which side of the equation she fell on.

"Laci Montgomery," he said, holding out his hand. "I've been watching your career for a while. Impressive."

"Thank you. I'm glad to be a part of the competition."

"And the exhibition, I hope?"

She frowned, turned between him and Taylor. "Exhibition?"

"Taylor hasn't told you?"

"I was just getting around to it," Taylor said, and to Laci's surprise he seemed mildly nervous.

Reggie shook his head and chuckled. "Well, then, I apologize for letting the cat out of the bag too soon. I would have expected Taylor to rush to give you the good news. After all, the exhibition will be the icing on the cake, and with him being in charge of it…" He trailed off with a shrug. "Well, it's going to be damn good for his career, that's all I can say."

"I have to pull it off first," Taylor pointed out. "You didn't give me much time." He spoke with a smile, though, and Laci could see that whatever the challenge was, it was not only important to Taylor, it was exciting.

"Too tight a schedule for you?" Reggie asked.

"Absolutely not, sir."

"Exactly what I wanted to hear."

"Just a sec," Laci interrupted. "The two of you have tweaked my curiosity. What exhibition? What's going on?"

"Reggie's had a stroke of promotional genius," Taylor said. "And XtremeSportNet is arranging for a charitable precompetition exhibition. Drum up excitement for the actual event, show off the surfers' talents, and have some positive societal impact. That kind of thing."

"Oh." She considered it. "That does sound like a good plan." The more coverage there was before the competition, the more press for the eventual contest—and its winners.

"But Taylor's being too modest," Reggie went on, "I've asked him to organize the exhibition because I know he has talent, too." The older man's smile was almost paternal. "Not to mention the fact that the exhibition dovetails into Girls Go Banzai."

She shook her head, confused, even as Taylor opened his mouth to speak.

Reggie got there first. "I assume he's told you that he's now in charge of Banzai."

"I was just getting around to that," Taylor said, his voice like ice.

Laci blinked. "That was what you wanted to tell me?"

"Uh, Morgan left this morning."

"Morgan was fired this morning," Reggie clarified. "Taylor is stepping in."

She eased the news through her head, telling herself it didn't matter. This was a new turn of events. There'd been nothing underhanded. He hadn't lied to her. When he'd come to Hawaii, he'd had no involvement in Banzai, just like he'd said.

She drew in a breath and nodded. "It sounds like an awesome opportunity."

"It is," Taylor agreed.

"Can we count you in for the exhibition?" Reggie asked.

Laci shrugged. "Sure. I guess. I mean, I'm already here, right?"

"Excellent," Reggie said, slapping them both affectionately

on the back as he stepped between them and continued walking. "It's perfect, of course. Perfect. At the very least, this is certainly going to put you on the map."

"I'm sorry?" Confused, she stopped walking, forcing him to do the same. Yeah, exhibitions often got good coverage, but this one was being thrown together so fast she doubted it would have any exceptional pull with the media.

"Cross promo with Danger Down Under," Reggie said easily. "That's the main thing we're going for here. With your Australian connection we should be able to get some serious buzz going. Probably get some shots of you in a bikini with your surfboard. That should rev the media up."

"Buzz?" she repeated, turning to eye Taylor, who looked positively mortified. "Is this your idea?"

"I don't—"

"Taylor saw the promotional potential the second I raised the idea of the exhibition. Sharp eye our boy has."

Her head was spinning. She opened her mouth, but couldn't speak.

"It's a shame we couldn't wild card you in down there, too," Reggie said, shooting what seemed to be a censuring look Taylor's way. "But at least Taylor tossed your name into the wild-card mix for Banzai," he added, and the words seemed to lodge in her heart, then twist like a knife.

Reggie leaned close, pressed a fatherly hand on her shoulder, apparently unaware that she'd completely lost the ability to breathe. "We're glad you're here, Laci. Really glad to have you on board. Your presence is going to do a lot for these competitions. And the competitions will do a lot for you, too."

She couldn't help it. And even if she could have, she doubted she would have stopped herself. But even as Reggie's voice droned in her head—even as Taylor muttered useless words about Laci not understanding, and how it wasn't what it seemed—she turned on her heel and raced down the beach to get as far away as possible from the man who'd lied to her, who'd used her once again.

The man she'd been stupid enough to believe really loved her.

Behind her, she heard the commotion that followed Reggie's sharp intake of breath. She heard the rise and fall of their voices. She even heard Taylor behind her, his feet splashing in the surf as he ran to catch up to her.

She considered lashing out again, screaming at him to get away from her. But she didn't have the energy. She'd trusted him, it had backfired and that explosion had ripped a hole in her. A hole through which every ounce of strength had escaped, spiraling away to nothingness and leaving her a little girl all over again. A little girl with a mother who took what she wanted whether she deserved it or not.

Laci wasn't like that, dammit. She wasn't like her mother at all.

But that's exactly what people would think when they learned that Taylor—the lying, scum-sucking creep—had put her up as the wild-card candidate for Banzai. And now—after they'd spent the weekend in bed—he suddenly wanted to cross promote her with Danger Down Under? It was San Clemente all over again, and the press was going to have a field day. The more Reggie promoted Banzai and the exhibition, the more the media would hang around. And the more dirt they would dig up.

That wasn't even the worst of it, though. What *really* hurt was that Taylor must think she was the kind of girl who wanted something for nothing, too. Otherwise, why not flat out tell her that he'd been responsible for her wild-card status? Why be all coy?

And why have that guilty look on his face when Reggie's unexpected presence made him reveal the truth before he was good and ready?

It didn't make sense.

And damned if it didn't make her heart hurt, too.

He had the power to do that now—to make her heart hurt and her eyes fill with tears. She'd gotten over him, or close to it anyway, and then this week, he'd wormed his way back into her life just in time to hurt her again.

For that, she hated him. Really hated him.

"Laci." He was right behind her.

"Get away from me."

"I am not letting you walk away from me over something that you don't understand."

"I understand just fine."

"No. You don't."

"Dammit, Taylor—" He grabbed her shoulders and pulled her up, then moved around so that he was facing her.

"Listen to me," he said. "Listen to me and then you can cut me off at the knees. But first, at least listen."

"It's San Clemente all over again," she said, voicing the words that had been spinning in her head.

"Why? Because you're a brilliant surfer and I wanted you in a competition? In case you didn't notice, that's what people who run competitions do—we try to get the best. And you know what? Even though you're right up there at the top, I told Reggie I didn't want you for Danger. He thought I was completely nuts, but I said no. Do you know why?"

"I haven't got the slightest idea," she said, itching to get away from him. She couldn't focus, and all she could concentrate on was being free and alone, because she couldn't think when Taylor was near her, and right then, she needed to concentrate.

"Because I figured it would weird you out. Having any sort of a connection to me."

That got her attention. "You think it's you? It's not you. It's me. It's what it does to me."

7

TAYLOR STARED at her, trying to understand what she was saying, but having no luck.

"Taylor, don't you get it? Don't you know how ashamed I felt? Like all the praise and accolades were coming at me because I'd slept with you? Do you think I'm that kind of girl?" Laci demanded.

"I don't," he said. "And neither does anyone who's seen you surf."

"But it's true, dammit. Can you honestly deny that you got me into San Clemente as a wild card because you were sleeping with me?"

He opened his mouth to do just that, then closed it again, a fact that she jumped all over.

"See?" she said, pointing at him.

He grabbed her finger, pulled her close. "No, Laci. *You* see. Yes. I made you a wild card at San Clemente because we were dating, but that only put you on my radar. If you'd been a hack—a sexy, wonderful, loveable girl who couldn't surf her way out of a swimming pool—I'd have kept on dating you, but I wouldn't have bothered getting you on the lineup. But you *were* good. Damn good. And you deserved a break. And you know what else? I was thrilled that I could give it to you. I was so stupidly, hopelessly naive that I was honestly excited that I was in a position to help out the woman I loved."

"Taylor—"

He held up a hand. "No. My turn to talk right now. Because you freaked and you ran, and I never really understood why. Because you have talent. Real talent. And I had no idea why you didn't want to show it off." He drew in a breath. "Maybe I get that the press embarrassed you, and the innuendoes were unfair. But we could have handled it together. We didn't get the chance, though, because you ran. And now you're running again, and this time it's because you don't trust me."

"Now," she said, "it has nothing to do with you. But I don't want anything to do with your exhibition or Banzai or Danger Down Under. I'm pulling out, Taylor."

"I know," he said, watching her face and feeling the loss as she broke away without telling him why. Because the reasons she was giving him weren't reasons. There was something else under there, something they had to get to because if they didn't, they could never really be a couple. San Clemente—this dark, abstract mess—would forever taint their relationship. "You need to talk to me, Laci. You need to tell me why."

"The hell I do."

He watched her face, looking into the eyes he'd come to know so well, and he saw determination. A strong resolve. And yeah, he saw regret, too. He moved forward and took her hands, trying with silence to express everything he felt for her. Everything he wanted for them. "Help me to understand. Please. I know you want this, Laci. More than that, you need it. You've told me you're hoping for a sponsor. And I know you can use the money. I've been following your career, remember? So why back out? Why not go out there on the waves and show what you can do?"

"And how nice of you to arrange all that for me. The press. The opportunity. It's so sweet," she said, her voice dripping with sarcasm, "to have it all dumped in my lap like that."

He couldn't help it; he snapped. "You know what? Forget it. You don't want this? Fine. You were never on my professional agenda, Laci, so it's no skin off my teeth. Reggie's the one making plans for you and Danger and the cross-promotion. That's been his gig from the get-go, and I realize now that's why he was so keen on having you be the Banzai wild card. And yeah, maybe that does suck. But it doesn't mean that you didn't earn the slot. One isn't exclusive of the other."

"So you think I should stay in," she snapped.

"Hell, yes. I think you'd be a fool to back out, but I'm not about to ask you to do something you're uncomfortable with. So if you're out, you're out, and no hard feelings. Not many, anyway."

She blinked in surprise, and he sighed. "I have to go. I've got forty-eight hours to put together a big, high-energy, heavily promoted exhibition that will draw a stellar crowd. The woman I love could help me do that, but I'm not asking her to. I want that to be perfectly clear," he said, stepping closer and making sure she was watching his face, seeing the truth there. "I'm not asking. I'm not forcing. I'm not even suggesting. What I am doing is leaving."

"Love?" she repeated.

He laughed, the harsh sound bubbling up from his throat. "Yeah, isn't that a pisser? I say I love you, and I have a feeling it's the last thing in the world that you want to hear."

And then he kissed her hard on the mouth, turned without another word and strode firmly away from her.

Laci carried the sensation of his kiss with her for the rest of the night and into the next morning. She woke up off center and still slightly baffled by his speech. He really didn't understand why she'd pulled out. He had no clue, and yeah, he was completely pissed off.

But even though he was angry—and even though her participation in both the exhibition and the competition could help his career—he wasn't going to push her to do it.

That could only mean one thing—he really loved her.

She'd known it. She'd believed it.

Now she'd seen it in action, and it humbled her. Humbled her because she couldn't return the same selfless act. She couldn't sign up for the exhibition and go through with the competition just to help him.

She couldn't do that and live with herself.

She needed to get to the top because of her surf skills. Not because she was dating the event promoter or because she grew up in Australia or because she looked hot in a bikini. That was too much like her mom, trading whatever she could for their condo. Whoring herself out for an advantage.

She shuddered, not wanting those memories to intrude.

She was in her bedroom, spread out across the bedspread, when a noise in the other room made her sit up. Drea or JC, she presumed, and because she wanted company, she hoisted herself up and headed out into the living area.

They both looked up when she walked in. "Feeling better?" JC asked. Laci had relayed the high points last night, pacing a hole in the floor as she'd run through Taylor's various crimes and misdemeanors. "You seem a little less steamed this morning."

Laci managed a tiny smile. "Considering the level of steam last night, a raging fury would still be less."

"Got a point," JC said.

"So have you calmed down, then?" Drea asked. "Are you going to do the exhibition?"

She frowned, looking at them both. JC and Drea were smart, competent women. Neither was inclined to do stupid things. Most important, neither was the type who would let herself be used.

With a frown, Laci focused on her friends, especially on Drea. "Why?" she asked plaintively. "Why are you doing the exhibition?"

"Are you kidding? It's great exposure."

"You, too?" she asked JC.

"Absolutely. Reggie called personally and said he could use someone with my creds. And if it promotes the competition, I'm there."

"But you don't have the creds," Laci said, back on Drea.

Her friend laughed. "Oh, thanks a lot. So nice of you to remind me that I'm the new girl on the block."

The words, however, were said without malice, and Laci kept pushing. "But that's just it," she said, wanting to understand. "It's like my wild-card slot. Reggie wanted me in so that it beefed up attention for another competition. That's using me. And it's me getting something for nothing. And you're in, why? To sell T-shirts and things because you look good coming out of the water?"

For a second, she thought Drea would snap at her with a smart-aleck comment, but her friend surprised her by answering seriously. "I look good on a surfboard, Laci. That's what this is about. For me, anyway. It's an exhibition, and I fully intend to exhibit my skills. It doesn't matter why I'm in. It matters what I can do." She shrugged. "Think about it."

Drea got up then, and she and JC headed out, leaving Laci alone in the bungalow to consider what her friend had said and to wonder if maybe her perspective on the world hadn't gotten all screwed up. And if it had, she wondered, could she fix it in time?

SHE FOUND him on the beach surrounded by beefy guys with tool belts constructing booths and platforms and a myriad of other structures to transform the beach into a media hub. Fans, reporters and other surfers hovered nearby, too, everyone scoping out the flurry of activity that would have an exhibition up and running in a heartbeat.

She hung back for a minute, waiting to see if he noticed her, but after she realized that he'd only see her if she had a walkie-talkie and a power drill, she took the plunge and waded in among the crew. They parted for her, a few catcalls and appreciative comments about the state of her ass echoing behind her.

When she reached Taylor, he looked up from a clipboard, his serious business expression softening once he noticed it was her. The expression behind his eyes, however, remained wary. "What's up?"

She sucked in a breath for courage. "Can I borrow you?"

He glanced around, his brow furrowing, and she knew that he was calculating all that had to be done.

"It's important," she said. "Important to me, anyway. And I'll be fast."

"Yo, Taylor," a hulk of a man holding a thick sheaf of plans said. "I need you, man."

Taylor nodded, but took Laci's hand. "Take five," he said, then steered her away from the crowd.

"I'm sorry. You have work, and—"

"You said it's important to you. I can always make time for you."

And that was just it, wasn't it? Taylor was willing to do all these things for her, and she couldn't even tell him why she wouldn't return the favor. Except, she could. *She would.* And she'd do it right then.

One more deep breath. Then another.

Concern flashed across his face. "Laci?"

She closed her eyes, and when she opened them again, she was composed. "I need to tell you why it bothers me. And why I won't do the exhibition or the competitions. I'm not pulling out to hurt you or muck up your chances to impress your boss."

"I know that. I don't need you to score points for me in my job."

"Right. It's just that—" She drew in a breath for courage, and then spat out what she'd never told anyone. "It's about my mom," she said. "Everything goes back to my mom."

She told him everything, barely even noticing when he took her hand, silently offering support as she described the way her mom had traded sex for favors, getting everything important in her life because she looked hot and put out in bed. "She never earned it," Laci said. "Not once. She thought that made her special. I thought it made her despicable."

"I'm sorry," he said, and though the words themselves seemed small and insignificant, coming from Taylor they meant the world to her. He pulled her close and kissed her forehead. "I'm so, so sorry."

"Now you understand?" It was so important that he understood. That it make sense to him why she couldn't do the exhibition. Why she wasn't competing in Banzai.

"Yeah. I get it." He crooked a finger under her chin and lifted it gently. "So what are you going to do about it?"

"Do?" she repeated, baffled.

"You're not your mom, Lace. And you do have talent. And you have earned all the good things that have happened to you. You've told me what's tripped you up in the past, and I get it. I really do. But it's not the past anymore. So what are you going to do now?"

"But—"

She cut herself off, her stomach twisting from an odd combination of excitement and fear. *He was right.* He was absolutely right.

She drew a deep breath and looked around. In the distance, she saw Drea and JC standing with some other surfers she recognized, along with a reporter she recalled from Channel 4. A cluster of crew members were staring their way, as well, shooting daggers in her direction since she was keeping them from their leader. A few fans had cameras pointed her way, although why they'd want a picture of her not on the waves, she didn't understand.

Because you've made it, the voice in her head pointed out. *You've made a name for yourself. And you made it on talent, kid.*

Yeah, she thought. *Maybe I did.*

"Laci?" Taylor prompted. "Are you okay? I have to get back to work, and—"

"I'll do it," she blurted. "I'll do the exhibition. The competitions." She drew a breath. "Everything."

His eyes raked over her, searching. "You're sure?"

"Positive," she answered. And then, with everyone from XtremeSportNet, the town and the fans watching, she planted a great big kiss right on the exhibit promoter's mouth.

And not one person thought less of her for it.

Amazing.

LACI EMERGED, dripping, from the water to the thunderous applause of the exhibition's audience. She stood on the sand, the surf breaking behind her and the crowd crowing and clapping in front of her, and simply smiled as the photographers snapped picture after picture.

Some, she was sure, would make the sports mags, along with the images the photographers had surely caught of her riding the waves, high on top, like the daughter of Poseidon himself in control of the mighty ocean.

She'd done great. No question about it.

And she could see on his face that the only one more proud of her than she was, was Taylor.

He stood beside the announcer's table with his fingers in his mouth, letting loose a string of wolf whistles while his boss, Reggie, cringed beside him, managing to look both pleased and mortified.

She crossed over to them, her smile so broad it hurt.

"You were terrific," Taylor said, twirling her into a spin.

"You were, you know," Reggie added. "I can practically hear the cash registers ringing."

"Good," she said without the slightest queasiness in her belly. "Pay my man more, why don't you?"

Reggie quirked a brow. "I'll have to consider that. At the very least, it would pay for the room you two need."

But Laci was ignoring him, intent only on Taylor's arms around her. "You really were wonderful," he said. "You know that, right? If nothing else, you proved you're here because of you and not because you have a brilliant, creative boyfriend."

"And sexy. He's desperately sexy."

Taylor flashed his slow and easy smile. "You're going to win Banzai."

She cast a glance over his shoulder at JC and Drea, both of whom were sending her thumbs-up signs. "Well, I have some pretty stiff competition. I guess we'll just have to see."

She slid her arm around his waist and leaned her head against his shoulder as the photographers started up again. The truth was, winning Banzai didn't seem that important anymore. The sting of competition had faded, and she'd lost the need to prove herself to herself.

Or maybe it was simpler than that.

Maybe she'd already won.

And with a smile, she held on tight to her prize, and then kissed him hard.

* * * * *

SURF'S UP
Karen Anders

To my Dad, who never let me down, ever.

Thanks to Stephen Pirsch for his expertise on crafting a surfboard from scratch. All mistakes are, of course, mine.

1

THE SUN cleared the horizon, painting the Hawaiian sky with brilliant hues of red and yellow. The colors of the sky over the aquamarine water almost took her breath away. It was, according to JC Wilcox, the best time of day.

The sand glowed with the first rays of sunlight, and the sun blazed a trail toward JC as it cast its reflection upon the water. The palm trees gently swayed with the morning breeze, and JC could hear the birds singing a gentle song.

Unfortunately, she wasn't here to commune with nature. She was here for serious business: competing against the top two female surfers in the XtremeSportNet Girls Go Banzai surf competition in Oahu, Hawaii. Laci Montgomery and Andrea "Drea" Powell were formidable opponents and just happened to be her good friends, as well as roommates. Laci was the wild-card newbie with something to prove and Drea was Rookie of the Year. Both women had just finished a phenomenal year and were being played up in the media as the ones to watch.

JC had known Laci for about fourteen months and had met her at a competition in San Clemente. Drea was an acquaintance who was fast becoming a close friend as all three girls had rented a three-bedroom, one-bath bungalow on the beach. With one bathroom, they had bonded quickly out of necessity.

JC attached her board to her ankle by its leash and splashed into the surf, watching the cresting waves farther out to sea. She paddled toward them, her focus on the wall of water creating what surfers called "the Pipe," a curling wave that just begged to be ridden. The pipe, now curling to shore, was how this stretch of the ocean had gotten its Banzai Pipeline moniker.

JC chose her wave. Hitting it, she turned her board into the cresting water as it rose. She popped up on her board doing a bottom turn, a sweeping move that allowed her to establish speed and direction. A crucial move if she wanted to set her rhythm for the ride as she settled into synch with the wave. Planting her feet in her sweet spot, the position a surfer placed her feet for maximum balance, stability and maneuverability, she felt the adrenaline rush through her as she slid under the breaking curl of the wave.

The wave zoomed over JC's head, a perfect tube of water weighing tons, but JC didn't think about that as she caught sight of Laci and Drea on the beach. For a second she was in perfect harmony, and then she saw her friends drop their surfboards and frantically wave. Before JC could figure out what they were alarmed about, something slammed into her like a breaking wave. JC flew off her board and went into the water, momentarily dazed. She felt the surfboard leash break as she was dragged toward the ocean floor. Steely arms came around her, easily pulling her to the surface where she sucked in a breath of air.

"Hang on," a deep, husky male voice said in her ear.

With her head ringing like a bell, JC went limp in the water to make it easier for her unknown rescuer to bring her to the beach. When they hit the sandy bottom, he effortlessly lifted her out of the surf.

"What the hell do you think you were doing?" Laci snapped. "She had that wave first."

At this point, JC felt the gritty sand at her back as he laid her down. She slowly opened her eyes—and got caught. Eyes that were a pure ocean-green and as vast, as deep and as ever-changing as the sea pulled her from her daze.

He leaned back slightly, his skin satiny and bronzed, his jaw tense. JC got a load of his hair—surfer-dude blond, a hundred subtle shades.

"Are you okay?" He was breathing hard, his chest heaving,

his hands going over her arms and legs, his smooth palms drawing goose bumps as they freely roamed her flesh. His brow, on a face JC had seen only in magazines, gracing surf posters and smiling out from a television screen, was creased in worry. Even all that exposure didn't prepare her for meeting him up close and personal. All her fantasies aside, the real thing literally stole her breath away.

He looked so worried, so upset that JC felt her heart constrict. "Zack Fanning. You're Zack Fanning."

"Looks like she's okay," Drea said wryly.

The concerned look didn't fade, nor did he acknowledge that he was a legend in his own time. A totally freaking awesome legend, until an injury took him out of competition.

"Are you okay?" he asked again, those expressive eyes boring into hers, searching them.

"I'm okay."

He sat back on his haunches with his head down. Softly he said, "I didn't see you. I swear I would never have snaked your wave."

JC sat up, unable to take her eyes off him. She wanted to touch him, slide her hand in his thick, wet hair and wrap him up in her arms. Even though he'd been the one to knock her off her board, she knew Zack Fanning would never snake a wave.

Integrity lined his strong jaw, covered him like a second skin. She'd watched him compete, seen what kind of surfer he was, and that gave her a lot of insight into what kind of man he was, too. She'd once had a desperate teenage crush on Zack Fanning, who was four years older. But even though she was now twenty-four, that crush had never abated.

Her infatuation with him became even more intense because he looked so good bending over her, his jaw covered in stubble that glinted gold in the light, his mouth soft and sweet-looking, and his eyes filled with her. She shivered at the look in them, as if he'd been dreaming and finally awakened to find reality much more exciting.

Laci bent down and dabbed at her forehead—JC needed the distraction.

"Oh, damn, you're bleeding. Let me get my emergency kit," he said, his voice an octave lower with more roughness. He got up off the sand, disappearing into the parking lot.

"Zack Fanning. Wow," Drea said softly, "he was a six-time world champion, and he's extremely hot by the way."

"We noticed," Laci said with a sarcastic tilt to her lips.

JC watched as Zack jogged back to the beach with a small first-aid kit in his hand. As soon as he reached them, he opened the kit and pulled out hydrogen peroxide and a gauze pad. Soaking the pad, he pressed it to her forehead. Those fathomless eyes met hers again and he smiled. It was like falling off a wave, just falling and falling into the deep, blue sea.

"How you holding up?" he asked, the pressure of his fingers gentle on her forehead.

"I'm okay."

"So you've said."

"I saw you in the Rip Curl World Championship Trials in Mexico the year you won. I went with my dad. It was so awesome. We drove down the coast to Oaxaca. I was there and saw you ride a fifty-yard smoker of a tube. That was so sick. You're the most awesome surfer I've ever seen," Drea said, her eyes bright with the memory.

Zack looked up at her, gave her a small smile and nodded. "I was feeling really loose and I had good boards."

"You're being modest, Zack," Drea said, matter-of-fact. "You were riding eight-foot waves like they were two-foot and ripping the biggest turns ever. Could I get your autograph?"

"Drea," Laci said.

Zack chuckled and removed the gauze from JC's forehead. His eyes met hers again and in them was something that she'd been feeling a lot lately—regret.

Her career at this point in her life was in the toilet unless she could pull a win out of the dangerous and awe-inspiring Banzai Pipeline. Her sponsor, Lexie, a giant conglomerate who sold clothing, gear and accessories, hadn't come out and said it yet, but she was on shaky ground.

Zack had already faced his worst nightmare, getting injured

and having to pull out of competition forever. He had been forced out; JC didn't have that excuse. *I so do not want to go out a loser,* she thought as Zack looked down to unwrap a small bandage to put over her cut.

JC's athletic talents had been apparent at a young age; now her star was about to go supernova and die out unless she focused all her energy into this make-it-or-break-it competition.

That was why any tingle she was getting from gorgeous Zack wasn't something that she intended to pursue. He gently pushed her dark hair away from her forehead, pressed the bandage to her head and then rose to his feet.

"Thanks."

He nodded. "Least I could do after ruining your ride and getting you tossed into the surf." He turned his head to look out to sea. The look on his face made her look, too.

Her stomach dropped. Pieces of her new, very expensive hot-pink-and-coral surfboard floated in the surf like some forgotten psychedelic flotsam and jetsam. It had been her best board and now it was toast. Just that morning, the airline had called and informed her that they couldn't find the boards that she'd put on her flight. What was she going to do?

"Oh, damn," JC said as she rose from the sand and made her way to the pounding surf. Bending down she picked up one of the pieces and stood there in dismay.

"This is my fault. I can't apologize enough. All I can do is to offer to handcraft you a surfboard and replace the one I broke."

For some crazy reason, she felt on the verge of tears. A broken surfboard wasn't the end of the world, but holding that piece in her hand she felt it was only part of her broken and battered dreams.

A warm hand settled on her shoulder. "Please, let me make this up to you. I've been crafting surfboards since I was twelve. I'll make you one that sings."

She felt his touch all the way to her toes and when she met those hot and devilish blue eyes, she fell all over again. She was not a fan of getting a board off the rack, so she nodded. "I would very much appreciate that."

"In the meantime—" he walked over and picked up his board "—take mine to practice on. It's beautifully balanced and wicked in the waves."

"I couldn't…"

"Yes, you could. *I insist.* Walk with me to my car and I'll give you a card so that you can come into the shop and we can get started on your board. Deal?"

"It's a deal," Laci said, coming up behind JC. "After all, it's only fair to make her a new board."

JC nodded and smiled at Laci. "A handcrafted board it is. Thanks for the offer."

"Thanks for being a good sport," Zack said as he walked with her up the beach. After reaching his car, he leaned inside and JC got a full view of his well-defined back, the thick, ropey muscles contracting as he searched inside his glove compartment.

"Finally."

Zack pulled his head out of the car and handed her a card. It had his name on it with images of custom surfboards underneath.

"Come by anytime you like. Just call to make sure I'm there."

Where JC tried to take the card, Zack didn't let it go. She looked up, drowning in those eyes once again. He smiled. JC smiled back and said, "And not out on the waves, knocking someone off their surfboard?"

His smile widened, a devastating smile that tingled through JC, stirring her blood and making her stomach drop.

"If they're as beautiful as you, it'll be worth the humiliation," he said softly. "Take care of that cut." He left then, getting into his car and driving away.

She walked slowly back to the beach to her friends. Drea was already looking over Zack's sleek board.

"Hello, ladies," a deep voice said at her left shoulder. JC turned to find XtremeSportNet's promoter, Taylor Dutton, standing in the sand. "Getting in some practice?"

"Yes, we are." Laci eyed Taylor and then turned away. JC saw the look of admiration in his eyes and a smirk.

A huge wave rolled to shore, and JC tucked Zack's card into her knapsack. Taking Zack's board from Drea, she headed for the surf.

JC WISHED to be anywhere but where she was. Cloistered in her sponsor's rented office space in Haleiwa, a surf town that served Hawaii's residents and delighted visitors with its quaint shops and cafés housed less than five miles from world-famous surf spots. She faced down two men who had the emotional IQ of a flea. She always thought of them as the California Boy duo. They had the same perfect blond hair, the same sharklike white smiles, the same barracuda personalities.

"JC, Lexie is concerned with your performance lately," Barracuda One said.

"I've been off my game, but I'm getting ready to roar back with a vengeance."

"We hope so," Barracuda Two remarked and he gave her his perfect shark's smile. "If you don't win this competition, I'm afraid we won't be renewing your contract. Lexie is looking for surfers who are continuously in the public eye."

JC walked out of their office and headed blindly for the beach, trying with all her might to keep her composure. She'd vowed she wouldn't cry in front of her sponsors and she'd kept that promise to herself, but now that she was out of the confines of the office and away from their unsympathetic eyes, uncontrollable tears slipped out.

She kept walking without thought as to where she was going until she walked into a solid living mass.

She didn't even bother to look up, but just mumbled her apology and waited for the mass to go around her. Instead she heard her name. "JC?"

Her stomach twisted with the recognition in his voice. This was the last person she wanted to see right now.

ZACK WAS TRYING not to think about JC Wilcox. It had been two days since he'd barreled into her in the surf and the impact of her—all of her—hadn't diminished.

He'd been disappointed when she hadn't shown up to claim one of his handcrafted surfboards.

But now, here she was, and he felt the reaction to her tingle through his blood until her tear-streaked face raised and her stricken eyes collided with his.

"What's the matter? What happened?"

"Oh, damn," she said softly.

He didn't give her time to protest or run away, even though he could see the intent in her eyes. He drew her over to one of the benches on the beach and folded down onto it.

JC looked to the beach longingly, but with a sigh, she sat next to him.

"Do you want to talk about it or should we just sit here? I'm not averse to putting my arm around you, strictly as comfort."

That made her smile just as he'd hoped it would.

"That was really lame, Fanning."

He chuckled and put his arm around her sunwarmed skin, telling himself he really was doing it for her comfort. Yeah, right.

"My sponsor is going to drop me if I don't win this competition."

To his surprise, she leaned her head on his shoulder and burst into tears. Being a guy, he wasn't that comfortable with a crying female, but JC's sobs were full of lost hope and so gut-wrenching—feelings he knew all too well. He turned toward her and pulled her into his arms.

With a soft cry, she wrapped her arms around him and just held on, dampening his T-shirt with her tears.

"Shhh," he said softly. "I know that's gotta hurt and be scary at the same time."

She nodded, and he let her cry out her fear and pain until she finally quieted.

She loosened her hold on him and all he could feel was regret as she sat back on the bench.

"I'm so sorry," she murmured, her embarrassment mirrored in her pain-filled voice. "You must want to run in the other direction as fast as you can. Can't blame you."

"I don't have any intention of running anywhere."

"No, that can be reserved for me. I just want to pack up and go home and forget I ever had a dream of being the best woman surfer in history."

"I think you're the best woman, period."

That got him a watery smile and a wry sidelong glance.

"Lame again?"

"Totally," she said, "but thanks for making me smile."

"My pleasure. It's a beautiful smile."

She turned those exotic brown eyes on him and he felt the world shift. She was the daughter of surfing legend Slade Wilcox and volleyball champion Lalani Wilcox. Her mother had been an Olympian and had died in a car accident when JC was sixteen.

A warning went off in his brain. A surfing woman was a bad bet in so many ways. But the warning dimmed to nothing. Instead of heeding it, he let his gaze slide slowly over JC's face. Her mother's Hawaiian heritage was strong there in the almond-shaped eyes, the high cheekbones and the summer-kissed skin. He let his awareness of her body seep past his barriers, giving the first rush of arousal free rein.

He couldn't keep his hands off her; he put his arm around her again and squeezed. Hell, he didn't need this, he told himself, not for a minute. But damn, she was so beautiful and so lovely. Too bad he was a sucker for a damsel in distress.

She was warm against him. Her dark eyes moved to his in surprise when his arm settled around her, and that soft mouth curved, a mouth that had been in his thoughts since the moment he'd laid eyes on her.

The trouble was he understood how she felt. He'd been through the gamut of emotions when he'd lost his own sponsorship and slowly declined in the ranks until he was just a memory. With his free hand, he rubbed at his scarred knee and shrugged off the memories.

"You're not going to prove them right, are you?"

She sat up straighter. "I know what they're thinking. What everyone is thinking. *She had such promise.*"

"JC, it doesn't matter what everyone is thinking or saying."

"They're saying plenty. I've read the stories in the papers. My father started training me when I was two. He made no bones about the fact that I had incredible balance and movement for my age. By the time I was six, I'd started competing in surfing competitions around Hawaii. Just a year later, I scored a sponsorship with legendary surfing clothing company Lexie. My breakout year happened when I was ten. I won several events that featured the best surfers in Hawaii in the seventeen-and-under category. *Surfer* magazine named me Breakthrough Performer of the Year."

"JC you've had a great career up until now."

"You're only as hot as your next ride, Zack. You know that. I can see the story now. 'JC Wilcox chokes at national competition. The girl who won the United Surf Junior Pro Competition can't bring it home.'" By fourteen, JC had won an astonishing nine national titles. In the majority of competitions she'd won she had been the youngest competitor in the field. In Australia she'd been the youngest-ever finalist, and she'd surfed in events all over the world. "'Looks like JC Wilcox's star has fallen hard and burned out in a flash.' That's a direct quote."

"Still, after all that success, you're not about to let your sponsors make you feel as if you're less than you really are?"

"Barracuda One and Barracuda Two? No. They have a lot invested in me and they're right. If I can't win this competition, maybe I don't deserve the sponsorship."

He rubbed the back of her neck and sighed. "It's tough, I know, but you're not out yet. How about we go get something to eat, since I'm starving, then we head over to my shop and make you a killer surfboard that will be unbeatable in the water?"

"Are you just being nice to me to get me into bed?"

"Who, me? Perish the thought."

She laughed this time, and he felt his heart soar. Standing, he took her hand and led her toward Da Kine. "Everything always looks better on a full stomach."

They entered, and Zack was greeted by his longtime friend and fellow surfer, the restaurant's owner, Kirk Murray. When he wasn't active on the circuit, you could always find him at his restaurant.

"Hey, man, I haven't seen you in a while," Kirk said. "Where you been?"

"Working for a living, unlike you, my friend."

Kirk laughed and eyed JC.

"JC, this is…."

"I know who you are. It's a pleasure and an honor to meet you."

Kirk nodded. "I know who you are, too. Radical waves you took in Fiji. That was some ride. You're awesome!"

"Thanks, but I didn't win."

"You should have. You got robbed," Kirk said as he took them to a table with a beautiful view of the ocean and the setting sun.

"Kirk!" one of the servers called urgently.

"Looks like I'm being paged. Enjoy your meal. It's on me."

"Kirk…" Zack protested.

"Enjoy. Don't forget you owe me a rematch at the pool tables."

"I won't."

After their meal Zack insisted on walking JC back to her bungalow.

"Feeling better?" he asked when JC stopped to pick up a shell for her collection.

"The fact that Kirk Murray not only knows who I am, but also thinks I'm an awesome surfer has boosted my ego considerably. I do appreciate this, Zack. The shoulder and the sympathy…but about the surfboard…"

"What about it?"

"It was an accident that you slammed into me. It doesn't seem right to hold you responsible for my smashed surfboard."

"The hell it doesn't."

"Don't get all indignant. I have another reason."

"You do?"

She reached forward to take the sting out of her words and grabbed his hand. "I'm entirely too interested in more than your surfboards."

He smiled. "What does that mean? I'm a guy. You'll have to spell it out for me." But he did know what her words meant. He just wanted to hear her say them, to solidify them in his wayward brain so he could get smart and not get more involved in JC Wilcox than he already was.

"Zack, I don't want to start anything with you that I can't finish. Besides, I'll need all my wits and concentration to win this competition."

"You think I'll be a distraction?" So much for using his brain.

She let go of his hand and walked a few steps away, the waves swirling to within inches of her sandaled feet. Her voice was low, but he heard it clearly above the sound of the crashing surf. "You already are a distraction."

He came up behind her, so close to touching her, close enough that he could smell her unique and heady scent. "This is really good for my ego, but I do have my reservations, too."

She turned to look at him over her shoulder, her mouth wry, her eyes snapping with barely concealed interest and wariness. Her eyes met his and clung, then dropped to his mouth. "Oh, you do?"

"My experience has been that surfer girls aren't a good bet. I've vowed to avoid them."

"Must be difficult when you own a surf shop."

"It hasn't been, until now."

The subtlest change came over her face and her lips parted. In invitation? Forbidden invitation?

2

JC WAS IN deep trouble. The deep-water, over-your-head kind of trouble. Zack stepped closer to her, his blue eyes mirroring the ocean in the diffused light from the beach. He was painted in shadows, shadows that delineated his broad, heavy chest muscles, the sleekness of his biceps and shoulders, and the power of his thighs roped in thick muscles.

Men. They were so damn beautiful with such strong, sleek lines, soft where they were supposed to be and oh-so-hard where a woman needed them to be.

"You're looking at me like you're having the same kind of problem. With me," she murmured.

"I am." He moved closer still, and her breath caught in her throat. He traced his fingertips down the side of her cheek, and then cupped her face with both hands, tilting her head back as he kept his gaze directly on hers. "That's good. I'd hate to think the way I feel was all one-sided."

The warmth of his hands made simple thought impossible. She couldn't look away from the hot intensity of his gaze. He had captivated her as soon as she'd met him in the flesh, but now, standing so close to him, the sudden lack of oxygen made her light-headed.

Her hand moved and slid into all that glorious blond hair, thick, surfer-dude hair that moved with the current of the wind as fluidly as he moved on a surfboard. It was soft and silky and felt erotic against her fingertips. His eyes darkened as her fingers tightened in his hair and she gently pulled him to her, pressing her body against his. Her mouth fixed to his, stunning her with sheer sensation. The kiss sizzled, sparked, smoldered.

She pulled away and looked up at him. "Lapse in judgment on my part," she said, her heart slamming against her chest wall. "Blame it on my terrible day and your sensitivity. I should get—"

He snagged her arm before she could turn away. "I think my judgment might be permanently impaired," he murmured. As he slid a hand around to cup the back of her neck, her eyes widened. She couldn't seem to resist. Before he lowered his mouth to hers, Zack's eyes told her he was as incapable of turning away from this as she.

This kiss was soft, seductive and luscious, sensations as unexpected as a sudden rainstorm on a hot day. It cooled and soothed and aroused all at once. She thought she caught a sound, something between a whimper and a sigh. The fact that it had slipped from her own burning throat amazed her.

But she didn't draw away, not even when the sound came again, quiet and helpless and beguiled. No, she didn't pull away. His mouth was too talented, too gently persuasive. She opened herself to it and soaked it up.

She melted against him, degree by slow degree. The first blast of heat had eased off, simmered into a deep, slow burn. She forgot about the competition, the pressure and her failures, knew only that she was tingling with life.

He tasted dark, dangerous, and her mouth was full of him. Her mind diverged toward taking, toward consuming, toward urgency. The civilized woman in her, the one who had her focus firmly embedded in her head, lost that focus as if it had swirled away in an instant.

Her mind reeled and she lost herself in the burning heat of his mouth, the feel of his smooth skin against her palm. An adolescent fantasy had turned into a very adult reality.

The warm surf pooled around her ankles, making her think of the liquidity of her response, the pull and tug of her desire settling into her sex like molten honey.

The ocean was her playground, her muse, her tormentor… The ocean—she couldn't think—the ocean, surfing, damn, the competition, she pulled away, backed away, splashing surf onto Zack's shins and thighs.

Her thoughts whirled with the possibilities of this man and she reached out for footing and found Zack's hand around her wrist, steadying her.

"Whoa," he said, staring at her, a mixture of hunger and shock in his eyes. But his touch only burned with energy that sizzled from her wrist to the part of her body that wanted him most.

The temptation was palpable and she wanted to sink down into it and let it take her so she didn't have to worry, have to guess, have to prove herself. It would be too, too easy.

But even as temptation beckoned, she knew why she was here back home in Hawaii. She was here to prove to herself once and for all whether she was her father's daughter.

And she'd known from the moment she'd met Zack's blue, blue eyes, he would be a distraction from what she had to do. She couldn't fail, and in the back of her mind, she told herself she had what she needed to get the job done. She was Slada Wilcox's daughter, winner of nine national titles. He was a legend and she couldn't let him down. The world was watching.

"Life has a way of kicking us in the ass when we're not looking, huh?" he soothed.

JC took a breath and looked out to sea. The exhibition to whet the North Shore's appetite for the Girls Go Banzai competition was in a few days and the competition itself was in two weeks. She needed the board and that was all. *Liar,* her mind said and she pushed it away.

"You have a very nice…mouth and you certainly know what to do with it, but Zack, I can't get involved here. I told you…"

"I know what you told me, but that was before we kissed."

He looked at her bare legs then, and concentrated on them. And such concentration. If he'd slid his finger over her thighs and ankles and down to her bare toes, she couldn't have been more aware of him. With his blue-eyed gaze moving over her so intently, she couldn't take a deep breath. Light-headed, she couldn't move, couldn't get enough air into her lungs.

"It happened. We kissed. Now, we have to focus on why we were together in the first place. You wrecked my surfboard."

"I did wreck your surfboard. That's true and I've offered to replace it. Now, I'm getting the feeling that you're trying to get me to back off by reminding me that what happened between us is my fault. I could take offense at that. Do what you want and send me to my separate corner. But I wasn't the only one here who was affected. I have to point out, JC, that you kissed me first."

He still had a hold on her wrist and he reeled her closer and smiled, his teeth flashing white in the darkness.

"I will concede that neither one of us resisted very hard." Zack continued when JC didn't answer. "You kissed me right back. Very nicely, too, I might add. So, the question you have to answer is, do you want to resist me some more?"

He let her go and folded his arms across his hard chest. She really didn't have a leg to stand on. She *had* kissed him first and it wasn't in her nature to back down from a challenge.

She reached out and grasped his forearm, feeling suddenly guilty for throwing all the blame on him. The feel of him anchored her as she drifted in the dark river of his eyes. "And you're right. I did kiss you first and did respond, so I can't really cast the blame totally on you. If truth be told, I should have been more vigilant when I was surfing. It's both our responsibilities that my surfboard was demolished. So, I think we should both work on restoring it."

"There's still time, if you wanted to get started tonight. It won't take long to shape it, but the fiberglass will take about two weeks to cure. That will give you the strongest board."

"I need to call my friends so they don't worry. Give me a minute."

She pulled her cell phone out of her pocket and walked far enough away from him enough for a private conversation.

"Hello."

"Drea, it's JC."

"Hey, we were wondering what was going on with you. How did your sponsor meeting go?"

JC could hear the hurt in Drea's voice and her hand tightened on the phone. "I'm sorry I didn't call. It didn't go well and I kinda lost it. Then I ran into Zack."

"Oh," Drea said. "You had a Zack attack."

JC chuckled, unable to hold on to her anxiety when talking with the always-upbeat Drea.

"You could say that. Now, he wants me to go to his workshop and help him craft my new board. I wanted to let you and Laci know."

"We appreciate that, but we sure understand why you didn't call us. I think Zack is dreamy. I'm sorry that your sponsor meeting sucked. We'll boycott them if you want us to."

This time JC laughed. "That's okay, Drea. They haven't dropped me yet."

"Okay. Call us if you need anything. I mean anything at all— a ride, clean clothes, condoms—anything."

JC laughed again. "Condoms, huh?"

"Have you looked at Zack, JC?"

She threw a glance over her shoulder to the man standing in the moonlight and thought that was the problem. She was too eager to look at every inch of him. Any other time she wouldn't have hesitated, but this competition was too important to become sidetracked. She couldn't deal with a man in her life right now, but she *could* deal with a just-sex relationship if Zack was willing. Who was she kidding? Men were always willing.

"Don't worry, Drea, I've still got hormones and my eyesight is twenty-twenty."

"Good, because you cannot live on surfing, my friend. Practice, practice and more practice makes JC a dull girl. Life is about balance."

"I'll take your advice into consideration, Drea."

"So we shouldn't wait up for you?" Drea asked.

"I didn't say I was going that far, sweetie."

"Oh, I almost forgot. Your dad called and wondered why you hadn't been by to see him. He said to stop by anytime."

Guilt twisted JC's stomach into knots. She'd been in Hawaii

three whole days and hadn't contacted her father. JC knew why she was reluctant to visit her father. It was all about her declining stats.

"I'll call him. Thanks."

She closed her phone and returned to Zack. "Let's go."

He smiled and came alongside her. "My Jeep's over here and, for your information, I have plenty of condoms at my house."

JC stopped dead and stared, her stomach jumping with anticipation. Zack turned and gave her a self-satisfied smile, and JC couldn't help but smile back.

"What's the matter, Fanning? Having a hard time finding a willing partner?"

He chuckled as he walked to his Jeep. "No. I save them for someone special."

Her stomach knotted. "We are going to work, right?"

"We are. I promise."

For some reason, JC wasn't thoroughly convinced. "Because there needs to be ground rules before we go forward with this."

"Ground rules?" Zack asked.

"That's right. No more kissing and no sex."

"Guess we won't need those condoms," Zack said with a mock leer.

JC laughed and slid into the passenger side of his Jeep. "You are a bad boy, Mr. Fanning."

"I try," he said.

When they pulled up in front of a gorgeous residence, all glass and wood, not far out of Haleiwa, JC turned to look at Zack.

"This doesn't seem like a workshop."

"My workshop is in the back. Fanning Surf Shop, where I sell my merchandise, is located in Haleiwa, but I prefer shaping and working here. I custom-built this workshop. Come see it."

He led her around the house to a garagelike structure attached to the place with a covered breezeway. She caught a glimpse of the ocean shining in the background along with a pool, hot tub and a beautiful two-level lanai.

He reached a set of wide double doors and threw them open. Following him into the structure, she heard another set of doors being pulled open and saw Zack way in the back, silhouetted against the night.

"I built it with doors on both sides. I can see the ocean when I'm working and catch a wave with a new surfboard to try it out. I also catch the ocean breeze and it makes it much less stuffy in here."

"It's impressive," JC said as she surveyed the area and took in all the neatly stored equipment and power tools. She could smell the blend of wood and resin and it was a familiar scent that made her long to be out on the waves with her board.

"I suggest we get out of these clothes."

"Excuse me?" JC said, whipping around to face him.

Zack laughed, the rat. "Making a surfboard is a messy business. I have some old clothes in the house that should fit you. Come on."

JC followed him out of the workshop and along the breezeway until they came to one of several sliding-glass doors. Zack unlocked it and stepped straight into the living room. The room was beautifully decorated in a modern style. Comfortable furniture looked inviting in the dark green-and-blue sunken living room, and sumptuous rugs covered the wood floors.

He turned to the left and started to climb the staircase, but stopped when she didn't follow.

"Come on." He gestured.

She moved toward the staircase and followed him up the stairs and down the hall to the master bedroom. Inside was a huge four-poster king-size bed, with a headboard featuring an ornate carving of banana leaves.

He rummaged around in a few drawers and pulled out a couple of pairs of cutoff jeans and two T-shirts that had seen better days. He threw a pair of shorts and a T-shirt to her.

"Try these on. The bathroom's through there."

He pointed toward an opening in the wall. Following his directions, she turned around and asked, "Where's the privacy?"

"It's a pocket door. It's in the wall."

"Oh," she said and pulled the door closed.

She quickly undressed down to her bathing suit and found

that, although the shorts were a bit big, they fit. The T-shirt was roomy, too, but would work for the job she was going to do.

When she opened the door, Zack was already changed and waiting for her.

"They fit okay?"

"Yes, fine. Thanks."

"I wore those shorts when I was younger and a little thinner."

She eyed his body and could see no fat on the man at all. He'd broadened through the chest, shoulders and waist as most males did. There was no mistaking that Zack Fanning was definitely a man.

"Let's go. Time's awasting."

She followed him once more through the jaw-dropping house until they reached the kitchen, where he grabbed two bottles of water out of the fridge. He handed her one and opened the other, taking a big swig.

"What kind of wood is this?" JC smoothed her hands over the dark cabinetry with uneven black stripes moving through it like waves.

"Zebra."

"It's beautiful, as is the rest of your house."

He shrugged. "I bought it when I was at the peak of my surfing career. It was a sanctuary, then. I guess it still is."

"Do you miss competitive surfing?"

"Yes, I do. After four years, I miss pitting myself against others who have the same skill and drive. I miss winning." He smiled wistfully and took another swig of his water.

"Where are your parents?"

"They're on the mainland in San Diego. My mom used to work for the navy and my father was a banker, but they're both retired now. They visit often."

"Why did you decide to stay in Hawaii?"

"I love it here and there's surf right out my door. When surfing ended for me, making surfboards became my business and where better to sell surfboards than here?"

He led her out still another door and they were back in the breezeway, heading toward his workshop.

He set the water down on a table in the corner and went to a wall that held blanks, the beginning form of a surfboard, and that was about all JC knew about surfboard-making.

"What are you? Five foot five and a hundred and twenty pounds?"

"Don't you know that a gentleman never asks a woman her weight?"

"He does if he's crafting a custom surfboard."

"You're absolutely right. That in itself is pretty impressive."

"It's what I do. I guess the airlines haven't found your other boards."

"No."

"That's fine. We have time to make this the best board you've ever ridden. Have you ever tried a parabolic?"

"No. I've stuck pretty much with the classic shortboard."

"In the Pipeline I would recommend you use a gun and with the twang of a parabolic it'll have you powering through those waves and sliding through the tubes like you were shot out of a cannon."

"Sounds great. I saw ten-foot waves at the Pipe just yesterday."

"That's nothing. They can get up to twenty or twenty-five feet. Okay, I'm going to go with a gun or what I would call semigun, which would be about seven feet. Sound good to you?"

"Yes."

He chose a board and set the blank on top of two board rests made out of wood specifically shaped to accommodate the board.

"The first thing that we have to do is remove the crust. All blanks come with a protective cover, but we want to get down to the foam. I use a planer to take us about one-eighth of an inch into the foam." He handed her both a mask and safety glasses.

Walking over to a workbench, he picked up a power tool. "This is a planer and is used to shape the board. I'll show you how it works and then you can give it a try."

JC nodded.

He set the planer to the blank and turned on the power. Foam dust kicked up, but the breeze pushed it away from her face and the mask protected her. She watched him move over the board.

It was like watching a master surfer—all sure movements and deep knowledge of what he was doing.

The use of the tool plumped his biceps and his shoulder muscles moved thickly under his skin. As he worked, a sheen of perspiration coated his skin. The wind kicked up again and ruffled his shaggy blond hair away from the strong column of his neck. Under the bright lights of the workshop, the blond stubble on his face gave him a primal, sexy look. She imagined that this is what the sun would look like if it was transformed into a man—all golden skin and golden hair.

She was moving back into that deep, deep water, but she couldn't seem to help herself.

He looked up and smiled. "Want to give it a try?"

She nodded and moved in front of him. He slipped his hands around her, pressed against her back. His groin hugged the curves of her behind, burning through denim to her. His hands covered hers, warm and strong, hands of an artisan.

"Start the planer off the foam. The bottom of the board is the most important. We want to make sure the rocker, the curved part, is shaped correctly." His warm breath tickled her ear and sent goose bumps all over her.

She nodded, pulled the trigger on the tool, and set it to the foam. They moved as one across the board. A board she would eventually ride in a competition that was the fulcrum from which her very career swung. It would either be an amazing rise to the top or the fall from on high. She almost would rather lose horribly than place somewhere in the middle of the pack and be just plain average.

She lost her focus and the planer went too deep into the foam. "Damn," she said, turning to look at him behind her. "Is it ruined?"

"No, just a rookie mistake that I can fix. No problem. Let's finish planing." They moved up and down the board in an almost sensual dance as the motion of Zack's hips and groin against her sensitized her skin and heated her body.

When they came to the end of the board, Zack signaled that they should stop.

He put the planer away and picked up the end of the board and checked down its length. "Looks good. Let's get the deck done." He turned it over and made quick work of planing the top of the board.

He took the time to eye the board again, then flipped it over to work on the rocker again and, presumably, to fix her mistake.

He picked up a curved tool and JC asked, "What's that?"

"You've never seen a surfboard shaped?"

"No. I just ride them."

"It's a sureform. When you want to do more subtle work on the board and a power tool is too much, you use this tool to smooth it out."

"You obviously know what you're doing. How long have you been shaping boards?"

"Since I was twelve. I got a job in a surf shop when I was sixteen. The owner gave me discounts on the boards and the job was flexible enough that I could make some money and surf when I wanted to."

"I already know so much about your career. Three-time world champion and inducted into the Surf Walk of Fame. Six years ago, you blew out your knee right here in the Pipeline. You retired two years later after falling in the rankings because of your injury."

His hands stilled and his eyes went a flat blue, like the ocean before a terrible storm. He smiled bitterly. "The good and the bad."

This was a difficult conversation and she wasn't sure why she was pushing him. She wanted to know what his real feelings were beyond that happy-go-lucky facade he obviously used to keep the world at bay. She knew all about that facade. She had one of her own. Tough JC Wilcox. "Yes, I wanted to know all of it. You've seen me not at my best and that gives you somewhat of an edge. I wanted to see the raw side of you."

"Will that make us even?"

She met his pain and anger with her chin up and her eyes clear. "No, not in the sense of tit for tat, but it will make us balanced. Just like the good and the bad."

"I don't like what happened, JC. It wasn't what I had planned for my life, but it happened and I moved on." He bent to the board again.

JC stared at him, at the wild gleam of pain in his eyes, the muscles that stood out as he clenched his jaw, the heavy rise and fall of his chest as he breathed.

"Did you?" she asked softly, her hand going to the top of his on the power tool. She watched, breathless and intent at the changing emotions in his deep blue eyes.

He breathed slowly and let it out. "It was…devastating to let it all go. I was lost for a while, but I found my way."

JC sighed, too. The genuine emotion that he showed her made her relax against a bench. The connection to the man made her tremble inside. "Do you miss it?"

"Yes, every damn day," he said, his voice low and full of meaning.

"I'm sorry." And she was. Her heart ached for what he had lost, but soared for his ability to put it in the past and move on with his life.

He shrugged. "It's the curve life threw at me. I've learned to take lemons and make lemonade."

"You're very talented, Zack."

At the soft tone of her voice he looked up and blushed. Her heart melted.

"Thanks."

As he finished up the board, she thought that she hadn't realized she could get so much pleasure from watching a man work.

"This looks pretty good," he announced.

Zack carefully ran his hands over the foam, clearly checking for bumps and abnormalities that he could smooth out. JC gasped softly, thinking about how his hands would feel moving over her flesh. The sensuous daze that had fevered her brain grew deeper. She was staring again and, worse, imagining what he looked like beneath that old, ratty T-shirt and sexy cutoffs. She'd seen him bare-chested on plenty of occasions. It had been the fuel for more fevered dreams than she could count. Something told her those youthful fantasies wouldn't come close to the images her very adult subconscious mind could conjure up now.

"Yes, it does from where I'm sitting." She paused to clear her throat. "Uh, the surfboard looks good, too."

When his attention didn't return to the surfboard, she folded her arms against her body and shifted her feet. "Time to call it a night?"

"Just about." He held her gaze for another too-long moment then made one last sweeping pull of the sureform.

She walked over to the planer and set it back in place.

He replaced the sureform and brushed at his clothing. When she came close to him, he brushed at hers.

"You okay?"

"I'm fine," she replied, the words coming too fast. How was she to tell him that it wasn't the fact that she was freaked over this competition or that she was going to lose her sponsor that had her on edge, but the fact that her "shoulder to cry on" was making her crazy? "I should be sleeping and planning out my schedule for the next two weeks. I should stop obsessing about seeing my dad and feeling like a failure because I can't seem to live up to his expectations. I'm afraid for the first time in my life of losing something really important and I don't know what to do about it. I shouldn't be standing here looking into your blue, blue eyes and—"

"Easy there."

He took her by the shoulders and squeezed; a now-familiar move that let loose all the butterflies in her stomach.

"That's way too much for this laid-back surfer dude to handle in one sitting. All I can say is it's totally understandable to be scared or nervous in tough situations. It's human."

She forced herself to lift her gaze to his. "The only thing that scares me and makes me nervous right now is you." Though she appreciated the way he'd immediately stepped in and grounded her, she wondered how he could be such a calming influence in one way, and total chaos to her system in every other.

"Yesterday I had a fully committed sponsor. Yesterday I had boards to ride. Yesterday, you were an adolescent fantasy and posters on my wall." She took a small breath, tried to square her shoulders and stand straighter. Mostly because what she really wanted to do was curl against his nice, broad chest and allow herself a moment, just a moment, of someone else sharing her burden and comforting her, making her believe everything was going to be okay. It was a moment she couldn't afford to take.

For far too long, Zack captured her gaze. In those heartbeats of time, she cursed her stupidity for inventing her hands-off rule. He put her hard-won equilibrium in jeopardy every time she got within five feet of him, but she didn't take her eyes off him. Just when she was losing her resolve to remain steadfast and not lean closer, his hands fell to his sides, but he didn't move away from her.

She was disappointed when he didn't drop his chin, lower his head, slide his hands up her arms and cup the back of her neck so he could tilt her mouth up to his to taste her again.

"That's how we get into these kinds of situations," he said calmly.

At first she thought by *situations* he meant the wild, uncontrollable attraction crackling and snapping between them, but when he went on, she felt her cheeks flood with color.

"You'll be moving forward with all your plans, thinking everything is going to fall in place, doing what has to be done, then, *bam,* you lose it, something big happens to change all that, to throw it off. Most of the time there is no warning. That's it. Things irrevocably change and you have to sit up and realize that what you had planned has to change drastically. You just hope that when that day comes, you can make a difference in your favor."

"And have you?" she asked, still struggling to put his words into the right context and not let her heart break for what he'd lost. She had to admit that the *bam* in her life right now was the presence of Zack in it.

He lifted a hand, as if he was going to caress her cheek. She held her breath, but he restrained the motion at the last second, let his hand fall back by his side. She had to work at not letting her shoulders slump in disappointment. She was the one who had set the ground rules.

"I hope so," he said, quite seriously.

Not the strong testimonial she was searching for.

Alarm began to creep back in, replacing the one-two punch of libido and fierce attraction. His honesty was refreshing and much better than fake bravado. "Me, too. Thank you," she said.

"For?"

"Being there." Her voice was thin and trembling at the sight of his smile. "Simple, isn't it?"

She didn't get the charismatic smile she had anticipated. Instead, his expression grew even more serious. "Your father loves you for who you are, JC. The great Slade Wilcox couldn't be any other way."

"My father is great. I should stop procrastinating and go see him."

"Would I sound pathetic if I begged you to take me with you?"

3

DAMN, he did sound pathetic.

And he'd opened his heart to her. Too late, the maneuver couldn't be recalled, he'd committed, and now she knew what he hid from the world, but he could be safe in the knowledge that she didn't know everything, and it would stay that way. He couldn't afford to completely open up to a woman with whom he probably had no future in Hawaii. So why did he even bother telling her so much when she'd touched a raw nerve?

She was so genuine, and he hadn't met that in a long time. There was comfort in knowing that she understood his pain. Now she also knew that he had idolized her father.

"There's nothing wrong with hero-worship. You wouldn't be the only guy I was with who wanted to meet my father. Sometimes that's the only reason they sought me out. Kinda hurt my ego a few times."

"I didn't mean that I…"

"Oh, I know that. I didn't mean to imply that's why you're hanging out with me."

"Good. Because it isn't. Don't mention my hero-worship to your father, though, okay?"

"I think he'll get it when you ask him to sign that poster you've been saving in shrink wrap on the off chance you'd get an opportunity to actually meet him."

"And where's the poster you have of me in shrink wrap?"

She laughed. "Touché. It's home on my bedroom wall so I can look at you. Drea's the one with the shrink wrap."

"And what about Laci?"

"Laci would never admit that she hero-worships anyone. It might ruin her bad-girl reputation."

He laughed. "Why don't you hop in my Jeep and relax while I pick up the rest of this and lock up. Do you have time to come back tomorrow and do some more work on the board? We can get the rails done and then there's not much to do after that. We could get resin on it by tomorrow or the next day."

"I'll make time. I enjoyed working on my own board."

She had enjoyed watching him. He could tell. Her eyes had followed his movements, her lips parting as if she was imagining how his hands would feel on her. He shook off that thought. They were going to remain platonic. It was the way she wanted it.

He had to admit that she did make him crazy and a bit nervous.

She nodded and left his workshop. Zack picked up, having a hard time keeping his mind on the tasks when all he wanted to do was rush to his car, slide his hand around the nape of her neck and draw her mouth to his.

After he'd turned off the lights and closed both doors, he started to head back to the front of his house and the Jeep, but stopped dead. She was standing on the beach, the T-shirt discarded, her shorts around her ankles. She was wearing a barely there bikini, her lustrous skin shining like diamonds in the moonlight.

His feet started to move, and just as they touched the sand, she ran to the waves and launched herself into the water. He walked to the edge of the surf and stood there looking for her as the warm water lapped at his ankles.

After a few moments, she rose from the waves and walked toward him. Water sluiced over her body and the bikini left most of her skin exposed, like a Polynesian woman in her primal habitat. Her nipples, dark and hard against the fabric, stood out in reaction to the air hitting her wet, slick skin. His brain short-circuited, his mind shut down and libido and hormones took over.

She walked up to him and stood there, breathing slightly from her exertions.

She reached out and settled her hand against his chest as if to keep him at bay.

He covered her fingers and pressed her there so he could slide his fingers beneath her wet hair at her nape and tug her mouth closer to his. And she didn't do a damn thing to stop him. "You made me crazy from the first second I laid eyes on you."

"You have to be the one to resist," she whispered, stepping closer.

"Why?"

"Because I can't."

She tasted like the heat of a Hawaiian sunrise and she softened beneath his hands and mouth with a sigh of surrender, allowing him to give up any pretense of trying to control himself where she was concerned.

The past, the present, warred in a tangled mess in his head and in his heart. He didn't even try to convince himself that taking a risk in this situation was smart. He just had to have her. He wanted to think he was well past that ugly part of his life. Clearly, he was not. He wanted her more than he'd ever wanted a woman before and that should have been a warning, but his need for her blocked out all common sense.

"Why aren't you resisting?" she murmured beneath his lips. She slid her arms around his neck and tugged him closer.

"Now why would I want to do that?"

His spirit soared and it almost hurt to feel this alive. "You were the one with the rules." He kissed his way along the soft line of her jaw.

She sighed and melted against him, stretching so that his seeking lips could better plunder her neck and the sensitive area beneath her ear. "My rules were rash and woefully imprudent."

His mouth found her throbbing pulse, wringing a gasping moan from her lips. It was enough to make him hard to the point of pain. And he wanted desperately to hear her make that soft, beseeching sound again. "Really? In what way?"

"Haven't you heard that it's a woman's prerogative to change her mind?" She gasped again when he sucked on her earlobe.

"I have heard that. How does it apply here?"

"Let me ex—" She broke off on a short moan as his fingers fanned wide, skimming her jaw, her throat, the slope of her shoulders. He cradled her breasts then let his touch flow downward over her ribs to her tiny waist.

"No need to explain. I'm starting to get it," he murmured.

She turned her head and planted kisses across his eyelids, along his jawline. Her fingers explored him, electrifying his senses and making him groan at the feel of her warm, satiny touch.

"Fast learner," she said, her voice soft and husky. "I like that. Why did I think I should deny myself this?"

"I have no idea." He turned her mouth to his and took it hard and fast.

She didn't miss a heartbeat. She ran her fingertips up the back of his neck and dug them into his hair, holding him where she wanted him, which was with his mouth against hers, lips parting, tongues dueling.

He curled his hands around the tiny strings holding the scrap of material around her hips and expected her to make a move to stop him. But she didn't. The thought that her resistance was gone surged through him until he was trembling with need and insistent passion. "This is crazy, you know that," he said, his breaths coming more rapidly as they tore at each other. "Tell me—" He couldn't hold on to the thought as she pressed her hands against the taut muscles of his back and over the hard globes of his ass, finally tugging his belt loops so he bumped more tightly against her.

"That I'm tired of being alone, tired of maintaining my me-against-the-world act," she said, her voice shuddering with desire, underscored by the reverent placement of her hot mouth on his neck, his collarbone, his chest, eliciting so much pleasure. His skin was so sensitized by her mouth that every place she touched, tasted, nibbled set him that much closer to the edge. Madness coursed through the night like a shooting star.

She shivered, and he wrapped his arms around her. "Are you cold?"

"No way! I'm burning up."

This time, as their lips met, every sense was heightened and he felt melded to her, filled by her. He was caught by the fragrance of her skin, the sound of her breath catching and the delicate lacework of her lashes as they swept against her cheek. She teased. She taunted. Their tongues met in a sensual slide, one along the other, taking, tasting. Soft moans filled the night air. He was drowning, and he didn't want to be saved. Reality would rear its ugly head soon enough. It always did. He wasn't going to hurry it along any faster than necessary.

She shivered again, and he knew it was from pleasure.

He wanted to throw her down on the beach, strip her naked and take them deep under to drown in the hot, liquid desire that rushed through him. So he had no idea where the tenderness that sprang up within him came from. He nuzzled the side of her chin, and then tipped it up until she opened her eyes and looked at him.

Her eyes were filled with an accusatory twinkle. "All of this is your fault."

Zack had to laugh softly. "Are we back here again?"

"Don't laugh. Woman's prerogative, remember?"

"How so?"

"Why did you have to be surfing at the same time I was? Your fault. Why did you have to be on that beach at the time when I lost it? Your fault. Why do you have to be so irresistible, sexy? And hello, hard?"

"I'd say that was your fault."

"Oh, man, is it?"

"You have to ask?"

"Men are too easy."

"Ha," he said, his mouth trailing down over her collarbone, latching onto her breast right though the cotton of her bikini top. Her nipple felt hot against his tongue and tasted of salt water. She groaned and arched into him. It was headier than sliding into the tube and feeling that wall of water roll over him.

"Ah, women are so easy."

"Let's make sure," she said softly. "Do that again."

He took her other breast and his knees buckled when her hand slipped around the snap of his shorts—and then they were gone, along with his underwear. He gave in and pulled on those tiny, tempting strings and the scrap of material covering her hot, pulsing sex fell away.

With quick hands, she pushed the T-shirt up his chest and off his shoulders. Together, they sank into the surf.

JC HADN'T PLANNED this. Not really. Yes, she'd come out onto the beach because she wasn't quite ready to go home. That terrible restlessness inside her demanded release. Is this what she'd chosen?

His hand moved up to her neck, and he released the string there and pulled her top down until her breasts were bare to the moonlight and his hot blue eyes. The breeze blew across her heated breasts and she cried out with the sudden sensation. Zack groaned, his eyes following the movement of her body. "Zack," she murmured.

He ran his palm over one dark tight bud and she cried out again, lost in the ecstasy.

"Damn," he murmured.

He bent his head and sucked her nipple hard into his mouth, the heat of it made her back arch off the sand, the grains rough against her backside only added fuel to her sensitized body. The heat flowed down her torso, zeroing in on her sex, forcing her to open her legs as she pushed against his body.

His hand found her sex and he pressed the pad of his finger over her. The double assault was too much and she cried out. He slipped inside her and she thrust against his hand, the tantalizing rock-hard length of him pressing against her stomach.

He looked into her eyes as he slid his finger out and back inside again. She gasped and gazed back, reveling in the punch of desire so raw it took what was left of her breath. It was heady, powerful stuff, knowing she moved him like this.

She groaned deep in her throat when he slid another finger inside her. She pushed up on her heels, forcing his shaft along the soft skin of her stomach. He groaned now, too, and bucked against her.

Reaching up, she pulled his head down to hers. She wanted

something more immediate than his fingers inside of her. She kissed him hard, and he returned it with equal fervor. He tugged her hands from their grasp in his hair and pinned them on either side of her, pressing his hard, hot chest against her water-slicked breasts.

The surf exploded against their bodies, the warm water drenching him, slicking his shining blond hair to a soft golden halo under the moon's silvery glow. Water sluiced from his body in rivulets, running over sleek, muscled skin.

"It's time to explore." He slid down her body.

JC tipped her head back as he let go of her hands. Closing her eyes, she tried to focus on feeling every sensation, every ripple of pleasure. She tried not to tremble so hard, but she couldn't seem to stop. The warm ocean slammed across her naked torso, brushing over her hot aching nipples like silk, sliding across her skin, drenching his hair, dripping off his jaw onto her as he continued his downward assault with his hot mouth and lips.

Her thighs quivered in anticipation of his touch. Even with the spray and the foam swirling and eddying around her body, she could feel his warm breath brush against her oh-so-sensitive skin. She wanted to sink her fingers into his hair, urge him closer and beg him to please put an end to the torturous wait. But he continued his exploration of her stomach as if he was feasting on her, gaining sustenance to slake his starving lust.

The sand, once grainy against her back, now softened with each wave that hit the shore and buoyed her.

He slid his hands slowly up her sides and back down to the crease where her hip met her thigh and she shuddered when he touched her pelvis and brushed his thumb over her swollen sex.

He pushed at her knees, nudging them farther apart and slipped his hands under her buttocks.

She sighed as, once again, his breath fanned across her inner thighs. And thought she'd scream at his teasing kisses and nips. A whimpering groan slipped from her mouth as he slowly drew his tongue along her aching flesh.

She realized her arms were still crossed above her head and she lowered them to brace herself against the shifting sand beneath her. She slapped her palms to the sand and arched her back with a strangled cry of pure pleasure. His hands tightened on her buttocks at the sound, and he moaned deep in his throat as his mouth teased over her sex.

Long moans, one after the other, poured out of her as his tongue rasped over her clit. Stabs of rapture shuddered through her, tightening in her core, as his tongue danced like a flame against her throbbing flesh.

The movements of his tongue took her higher as the waves slapped against her, stimulating every nerve ending in her body until he pushed her over.

Wave after wave continued to rock through her. Then he did something no other man had ever done. He waited, patiently until she dropped ever so slightly from the peak and his tongue took her again. She climaxed so hard, her body convulsed in pure pleasure.

He slid his body up along hers, linking his hands with hers on the sand.

"You were…" She had no words. Her brain could not form the sentence. Her thoughts scattered as the aftershocks trembled through her. She was still trying to come back to her senses. "That was… You need…"

"Shh," he told her, then pulled her arms up around his neck and kissed her.

She was yielding in his arms, grateful for his strength, his guidance, his support of her. Any moment now she'd rally, she'd be a more vigorous partner, giving as well as taking…but right then, his kisses were almost as consuming as his tongue had been. Later…later she'd return the favor. He didn't seem all that insistent anyway. And this felt too good. Nothing had ever felt this good.

He was both tender and intense, making her feel both protected and coveted at the same time. He tucked his hips against hers, still kissing her deeply, twining his tongue along hers as he slid his hands down and pulled her thighs up over his hips, pinning her to the sand. "JC…." he murmured against her lips. "I don't want to stop, but—"

"Then don't." She buried her fingers in his wet curls and tugged his mouth back to hers.

"Protection," he said, his body tensing as she hooked her heels behind his thighs.

"Damn. I totally didn't think…"

He lifted his head, looked her in the eyes. "I have some at the house."

The depths in his very dark eyes stole her breath. She'd never had a man look at her with such need before.

"Go get one." He went to rise, but her arms brought his eyes back to hers. "And Zack, use those beautiful thighs and run, because I need you inside me, right now."

It was a few long moments before he returned. His hot body dropped back onto hers. "I think I broke the sound barrier."

"You did good," were the only words she could muster. "Please, Zack." The intense feeling she was experiencing was as thrilling as it was intimidating. But now was certainly not the time to worry about that. She needed….

Her thoughts scattered as he slid slowly, fully and completely inside her.

She dug her fingers into his shoulders and locked her ankles more tightly behind him as he thrust. His broad palms covered her hips, guiding her into him. She arched, moaned and, when he began to move faster, she matched his pace.

She'd never experienced this kind of basic, earthy, raw…almost primal lovemaking.

She wrapped her arms around him and held on, both of them lost in the pleasure as his thrusts grew deeper, faster. She wanted to linger, so she could savor every second, immerse herself in every feeling, every sensation, but she couldn't even keep her eyes open to watch him. He was taking her up to the edge again and she could only ride the wave in surrender to the powerful emotions tingling through her. *This is just sex.* Somewhere in the back of her mind, she reminded herself of that. Or tried to.

Every instant they touched and kissed forged a binding union, a bond like no other. Ludicrous. She was relieved that she hadn't blurted out her feelings, as she was certain when it was all over, she'd laugh at herself and her silly emotional reaction to what was just extraordinary sex.

And it *was* Zack Fanning, after all. Her dream finally come to life. So surely she was just tangling fantasy with the moment.

Thoughts scattered completely as he slowed, and she could feel his body poised in taut control to prepare for that last exquisite push. It was enough to send her over. Waves drove them across the sand; water poured over her sweat-slickened torso as she gasped for air and returned each thrust with equal force.

He released a harsh groan of surrender then and gripped her hips, rocking her in time to each frantic upward surge of his thick shaft within her. She gave herself over to him, reveled in his shuddering release, tightening around him to give them every last ounce of pleasure.

He was shaking as he slid from her body and let her legs drop from around his waist. He held her tightly against him as they both fought for breath.

It felt good being in his arms, she decided. Held so tightly, both cuddled and coddled. It wasn't like her to accept that from anyone, most especially like this. She'd fought so long and hard for independence, it had carried over to all aspects of her personal life, including intimacy. So why she so willingly accepted him, his surprising tenderness, she had no idea. She chalked it up to…the stress. To the fantasy. Because her reality had never been like this.

He must have felt some nuance in her body because he strengthened his hold slightly, and then slid his hand up to cup her chin.

"Hey."

That brought a smile to her lips. Men. Such a way with words. The silver-tongued devils. But she sobered at the bewildered look in his eyes. She wanted to make a silly comment, but the unexpected warmth she saw there stopped her from teasing him. She felt much the same way and wondered if he saw that in her eyes. "Hey, yourself."

"That was…" His words just died, but he held her gaze, his blue eyes deepening in a way that jacked up her heart rate again.

"Yeah," she said softly. "It was."

He rolled and stood. Before she could even move, he'd gathered her into his arms, settling her against his chest. The soft places on her easing against all the hard planes on him. It felt remarkably fantastic...and far too perfect.

"I can walk."

"I know that."

He moved forward and, for once in her life, she let herself lean just a little bit more.

4

THE SOUND of the waves woke her. She shifted against the wall of hard, warm muscle and came face-to-face with a sleeping Zack Fanning.

Wow. Awake he had all that intensity working for him, but asleep, those blue eyes shuttered, she could study his arresting face. His thick, tousled blond hair lay on his stubbly cheek and forehead. JC could see red in his beard and in the long eyelashes that lay thick on his cheeks.

She reached out and pushed his hair off his forehead, the strands silky against her fingertips.

Gently she slid away from him when he stirred. She didn't want to wake him. She found his robe behind the bathroom door and shrugged into it. Looking for her phone, she realized that she must have left it on the beach. She stepped outside into the beautiful day. The ocean lay like a ribbon of blue all the way to the horizon. She wished she had her board and could be out on the waves, riding free and easy.

She walked to the sand and found the shorts she'd been wearing. Digging through the pocket, she found her phone. As she pressed Laci's cell number, she started to pick up the clothing that had been discarded the night before.

"It's about time. Did you work through the night to get your board nice and stiff?" Laci said slyly.

"You, my friend, are very bad."

"Well, dish. Is he as good in bed as he looks?"

"Better."

"Damn. I'm mad that you're getting some and I have to just look."

"Who you looking at?"

"It's not exactly a smart move."

"So, here I am sleeping with Zack Fanning when I should be getting my stuff together, practicing and watching my calendar to make sure I didn't miss anything. Why not humor me with your blunders."

"I hear you."

"You know I would never say a word."

"It's Taylor...."

"Dutton? XtremeSportNet's promoter? I wonder what Reggie would think of that."

"I'm discreet. I haven't been able to stop thinking about him since we met in San Clemente."

"Oh, man," JC said.

"Yeah, you can say that. He's all man. That's nothing. Drea is getting pretty chummy with her sponsor, Kirk Murray."

"I met him last night at Da Kine. Even though we haven't known Drea for very long, she's a pistol. It seems he's just Drea's type, huh?"

"Yeah, hot, muscled and gorgeous. So, are we practicing today? The exhibition will be here before you know it."

"Yes, I'm just getting my stuff together. I'm going to make breakfast and then see where I am. Zack thinks we can finish shaping the board today."

"Unless something else comes up between you."

"Stop it, bad girl. I'll call you, okay?"

"Got it. Stay cool."

JC went back up the beach and into the house, dropping the clothes in Zack's laundry room and folding up her bathing suit and tucking it into a plastic bag before putting it into her purse.

She went into the living room to look for the remote as she liked a little noise while she was cooking, and noticed a room off to the side. Curious, she went to look inside and saw that it was some kind of production room. In it were clothes racks and fabric along with a sewing machine. She picked up a folder and started to page through it. There were plans in it to expand Zack's business, budgets and projections, investors' names listed, and trademark paperwork.

Flabbergasted, JC smiled, thinking it was a good thing he was going to expand…her thoughts abruptly halted when she saw the date on the paperwork. Sitting down at the desk, she discovered that these plans were four years old. All this had been sitting around for four years?

Why?

She walked up to the racks and realized that the clothes had not been sitting here for four years. They were clean and some of them still had pins in them. She pulled a short and halter set off the rack and swore softly under her breath. It was beautiful, with blocked colors. The little tag on the front said Color Babes. She pulled other clothes off the rack and saw labels that said Deepfish. There was stuff made for boys and men with labels printed with Hook, Line and Sinker and Starfish.

JC looked up at the wall and saw a sign done in blues and greens that said, Fanning Surfboards and Koi Apparel.

"What are you doing in here?"

JC jumped and turned. Zack stood in the doorway and for the first time since she met him, he didn't give her that easy smile. His mouth was tight, his eyes stormy.

Uh-oh, this was a battleground and she'd just walked into it.

"Just looking around."

"Is this what you do when you come to someone's home? Snoop?"

"I wasn't snooping. I was going to make breakfast."

He stalked into the room until he was almost on top of her and she realized how very tall he was. "Well, you lost your way to the kitchen, Goldilocks. The porridge is in there."

His proximity was making it really difficult to concentrate on what he was saying. Her body was getting the message loud and clear, but it had nothing to do with making breakfast.

She put the clothes back on the rack and deftly moved to one side and away from him so she could breathe.

"The clothes are beautiful. Did you design them?"

He glanced at the racks and then at her, then down at the desk and his face tightened. "Did you go through my papers, too?"

Zack moved around the desk and once again stood close to her. Bracing herself, she studied him. Up close like this, almost as close as they'd been last night when he'd kissed her, it was impossible not to get caught up in his intensity. He didn't even have to try that hard. No one who witnessed those laser-beam eyes of his or the dangerous way he smiled could be under the impression that he was nothing but a laid-back surfer dude.

"Tell me something, Zack."

"Sure," he bit out. "Apparently I'm an open book to you."

"What are you waiting for?" JC asked.

ZACK SIGHED and left.

In the kitchen he set up the coffeemaker and started it, ignoring JC as she stood in the kitchen doorway, staring at him.

Could a woman look any more beautiful? She'd been romping around in the ocean with him yesterday, was wearing his old bathrobe now and yet she looked fresh and breathtaking.

He'd admit that it had been a long time since he'd let a woman in his home, let alone in his heart, but in one night this woman had gotten a foothold and it spooked him. He had liked his life the way it was. He lived in the now, not in the past and not in the future.

"Are you going to give me an answer or duck the question? What are you waiting for?"

"And if I duck, JC? What then?"

"I'd have to wonder why fearless Zack Fanning was ducking anything."

"Fearless." He shook his head and met her eyes. "There are things to fear, JC. I found out the hard way."

"So, are you afraid of expanding your business?"

"Not afraid. I'm cautious."

"*Cautious?* It's been four years since you made all those

plans, Zack. From what I can tell, they look great. And the clothes…they'd sell like crazy to the surfing and nonsurfing crowd alike. They bridge a gap between the two. All you really need is a marketing plan."

He opened the refrigerator door and pulled out eggs and bacon and set them on the counter.

"Do you know what it's like to lose your dream, JC?"

"Not yet."

"Then don't tell me what I should or shouldn't do. You can't even make up your mind whether to face your father."

Her eyes clouded and her lips tightened. She turned on her heel and started to walk away.

Damn. He was feeling threatened, but that was no reason to attack her. She was simply asking questions he should have been asking himself a long time ago. He should let her walk, but after last night he couldn't.

He lunged for her and caught her loosely around the waist. He said, "I'm sorry. That was uncalled for. I…appreciate what you said about my designs. I understand where you're coming from, but can we just agree that I'm not there yet?"

He'd lost himself when he'd lost surfing, had wallowed and, with every ounce of his strength, he'd pulled himself out and started making boards. His dream had disappeared on that stormy day in December when he wiped out and hit the rocks so hard it had shattered his knee. He'd been lucky he could still walk.

Now he lived by being careful not to want too much, need too much. Yet, standing in his sunny kitchen, he found himself thinking about JC and where they could go with what had been forged between them last night.

And the thought of what he wanted terrified him more than anything had since the day he'd lost his dream. JC was a surfer, and surfers went where the waves took them. He couldn't follow. It would be better for them both if he just let her walk out of his house. But he owed her a board and maybe an explanation.

"I'm sorry, too. I was snooping in your house and talking

about things that really are none of my business. I barely know you. It's that, you are so talented and I hate to see you waste it."

"I had plans once and they didn't work out. Now I'm more cautious about what I want, JC. That's it." Except in her case he hadn't been cautious at all. He'd tried to convince himself that her only appeal was physical. That the bond humming between them was nothing more than sexual. But the memories of JC seduced him. He believed she had the courage to go where she needed to go. He, to his shame, did not.

She turned and looked up at him. "Trust me. You will know when the time is right. Just...don't wait too long or it'll pass you by."

That spirit lured him, spoke to him in a language he heard distantly and longed to understand.

She lifted her face to his, her eyes unguarded and warm, daring him to leap into the unknown with her.

She left him defenseless.

A tendril of her hair tickled his nose, brought with it her scent, her sweetness. With her in his arms and her scent lingering near his mouth like a voice calling him, he couldn't fight her, couldn't fight himself. No longer wanted to.

She asked him for trust.

He didn't know if he could trust.

Didn't know if he had it in him to forget the lessons he'd made himself learn through the years since his accident. To depend only on himself. To look before he leapt. He wanted to lower his barriers and trust her, but caution, the ruling principle of his life, argued against it.

But caution, ah, caution held you back from taking something that would be worth the risk, caution paled against the lure of JC's spirit.

"I'll try," he muttered into the curls tempting his mouth. "It's not the answer you want, JC, but it's the best I can do."

"That's all I want, Zack," she whispered. "The hope that you'll open yourself to the possibility. Risk is what it is—not good, not evil, either."

Taking her hand he led her up to his bedroom, to the big bed they had slept in together. The room was filled with the memory of her already. He tugged her to the bed, pressing her down as he folded on top of her.

There was more here than the pulse of desire. More than the craving of his body.

There was something outside his comprehension, beyond his understanding.

Risk.

For her. For him.

Tantalizing.

Terrifying.

In that strange light, as he knelt on the bed, his right knee close to the curve of her waist, wonder moved in a deep tide through him.

"This is something special, Zack. Isn't it?" There was wonder, too, in her eyes.

"I suspect that it is. I'm afraid to look at it too closely," he murmured, touching her face, pushing away soft brown strands. "Something else entirely." He twined his fingers in her hair, the rich mass spread across his rumpled sheets. "Did you come to chase away my fears?"

He lifted one thick strand, letting it run through his fingers like silk.

"How could I? I have my own." She stroked his mouth, and he caught one fingertip gently with his teeth, tasting her. She turned toward him, one knee raised, the robe sliding down her thigh.

"What do you want?" He raised her hand to his mouth and kissed her palm.

"Whatever you want," she whispered, the honeyed sunshine of her voice glowing inside him, blending with the tide swelling in him, pushing back the doubts and pain.

Her voice offered entry to paradise when he'd thought to linger forever at the gates, locked outside.

With the backs of his knuckles, he edged the terry cloth wider, tugging at the belt across her waist. Parting the robe, he stared down at the delicate flare of her hips, the threshold to her sex and up to her full, tantalizing breasts.

"Are you just going to look?"

"Are you rushing me?"

"I wouldn't dream of it. Just asking a simple question."

"You're nudging."

He traced his fingertips across her abdomen and she sucked in a breath. He felt her hands on him, climbing up his ribs, smoothing across the undersides of his arms. Easing himself down beside her, he lay facing her, watching her eyes change, darken, as he passed his forefinger over her inner thigh, brushing against her in minute sweeps closer to her intimate heat.

"I want what we had last night. The passion," he whispered, letting his breath caress her stomach.

"I want that, too." Her hands came up to cup his face, her thumbs caressing along his cheekbones.

He slid his thighs over her restless legs, holding her still as he reached into the nightstand quickly for a silver packet. "Let's go with that then, sweetheart."

He slipped off his shorts and his shaft sprang free. Before he could complete the sheathing, her hands were on him, pressing him back against the headboard. She found his rigid nipple and nipped at the sensitive disk, and that stab of erotic sensation spiraled all the way down to his groin.

She kissed along his torso to his belly and kept nibbling her way lower with soft, delicious bites and the scrape of her teeth along his heated skin. She took him in her hands, her grasp snug as she measured the length of his cock in long, firm strokes that had him gritting his teeth in a painful kind of pleasure. Her thumbs grazed the lubricated head of his penis with every pass, drawing a fierce climax closer to the surface.

"JC," he said, his voice a deep, husky growl.

Slowly, she curled her tongue over the broad head of his sex, then licked and nibbled her way up and down his cock. Softly, leisurely, she pleasured him with small, appreciative sighs and moans that made him writhe beneath her. Just when he was certain he was on the verge of climaxing, she finally parted her lips and enveloped him in the wet heat of her mouth.

His nostrils flared, and savage lust reared within him as she took him deep, working his thick, solid member with her lips and tongue, her fingers wrapped around the base.

Her mouth slicked over him and his hips bucked beneath the onslaught and he almost lost control.

He pushed her up and away from him, sheathing himself as quickly as he could. Straddling her, his breathing ragged, he tugged the hot bud of her nipple into his mouth. She arched wildly beneath him, shuddering as he slipped inside her. He impaled her on the moment of her pleasure and then drove her higher as he wrapped her legs tightly around his waist and slid his hands under her thighs, lifting her to accept each deep thrust.

He wanted to make this last forever, wanted to stay with her in that burning darkness, consumed.

But his hunger for her betrayed him. As he held on to her smooth flesh, pushing himself toward the edge with an urgency he hadn't dreamed of, her whimper sent him tumbling over into the sun.

He watched her flash and burn with him, her eyes wide and filled with him until that final second when she arched into him, panting, her eyes closed, and he followed her, losing himself in her completely.

5

IT DIDN'T take long for Zack and JC to finish JC's board. Dressed in Zack's clothes again, she ran up to his shower to wash off the grime of the workshop.

When she came out of the shower, Zack was sitting on the bed. He had the beautiful blocked-color halter top and shorts in his hands.

"Since you love them so much. They're yours."

"Are you sure? They're almost too gorgeous to wear." JC took the garments from him and smiled. "I don't suppose you have a blow-dryer here, do you?"

"I do. I sometimes use it in the workshop. It's under the sink."

JC made quick work of getting herself ready for her photo shoot. She was so glad to see that the shorts had a built-in panty that made underwear unnecessary. Once she was dressed, she picked up her dirty clothes, stuffing them in a bag Zack gave her. Zack took her over to the Pipeline where she was shooting.

The waves were huge and as JC walked out to the crew, her palms started to sweat. Zack followed and dropped into the sand to watch.

"Are you sure you won't be bored?" she asked.

"No. You don't have a ride back to your bungalow. I'll wait."

"All right. Thanks."

Lindsay Michaels walked up to JC. She was the photographer. "There's no one here from Lexie."

"Wow. That's crazy."

"I love what you're wearing. Where did you get it?"

"That guy over there—" JC pointed to Zack "—designed and made it. He's Zack Fanning."

"Nice. Is he a designer?"

"He doesn't think he is. I wish he'd get a clue and expand his surfboard business."

"I heard that Evan Banks is looking for an investment."

"Really? The real-estate mogul?"

"Yep. So, what are we going to do about the shoot? Cancel?"

ZACK WATCHED as JC took over organizing the shoot. When a representative from Lexie showed up forty-five minutes later, the shoot was almost over. Meanwhile, Zack was impressed by JC's ability to organize everything.

The more he got to know JC Wilcox, the more he admired the woman. When she walked over to him after the shoot, he didn't want to drive her back to her bungalow. He wanted to spend the rest of the day with her.

"Do you have to go back to your bungalow?"

"Yes, I need to get my…your board and do some practicing. There's still plenty of light and plenty of waves."

"How about I come with you? I've got a waverunner. Get you out to the waves without tiring you out."

"You want to help me practice?"

"I do."

They spent the rest of the week practicing, and Zack crafted two spare boards for JC, in case the first board he'd made for her got damaged in the competition. Zack went to the exhibition. Every day they spent their time making love and he helped her practice. It was the best two weeks of his life. But as the competition loomed, so did his unrest.

It seemed that JC was also getting anxious about the competition. She often stared out at the ocean and studied the waves. They'd been to the Pipeline several times to practice and she'd had some trouble with the waves, but he kept encouraging her.

On the day before the competition, JC lay curled next to Zack. He played with her hair, letting the silk slide through his fingers, wondering what would happen once the competition was over and JC had gone on to the next event. It hurt to think about her missing from his life.

But it would be selfish of him to ask her to stay.

"What are you thinking?" she asked softly.

"That the competition is over tomorrow and you'll get to prove yourself to all the skeptics."

"You think so?"

"I know so," he said. "You have what it takes. Remember I've been out with you every day and seen you. I know you're talented."

"I'm not so sure of that. If I pulled out of the competition...."

"Pulled out?" He sat up. "What are you talking about?"

"I'm afraid," she said in a small voice. "Afraid that I'll never live up to my potential. That all the people who said I didn't have half the talent of my father are right."

He squeezed her shoulders gently. "JC, they're not right. You have to believe that. You're going into the Pipeline tomorrow. You can't have any doubts when you're facing fifteen-foot waves."

"You wouldn't want me to stay with you," she teased.

He swallowed. He wanted that, but the thought of giving himself over to his feelings scared him deep down inside. JC had to move on and he had to let her. That he wouldn't have to delve too deep came as a relief. The risk of giving his heart was one that was just too big right now. He had to let her go and chase her dream. His was long over.

"Then you'll never know whether you could have achieved everything you possibly could have. I don't want you wondering that your whole life. Do you?"

"No."

"Good. I *had* to leave surfing, JC, but you can go all the way."

"All the way," she said, smiling up at him. "Hey, my father invited me to a party tonight."

"You talked to him."

"No, he left another message at the bungalow. I'm not sure why I'm reluctant to face him. It's not that he'll ever say to me that he's disappointed in me."

"Don't be that way, JC. I'm telling you that your father won't be anything but proud of you."

"You're right. Will you go with me?"

"Yes, I will."

JC HAD BEEN under the impression that her father's party was going to be a small gathering. She had been totally wrong. So she was glad that Zack had taken her home to change into a cute skirt and pretty T-shirt. As they made their way through the house to the open patio, a woman placed leis around both her and Zack's necks. The back of the house was lit with white lights, illuminating the palm trees and foliage. The hot tub, whirling with frothy white water, hummed as the bartender handed out colorful cocktails to guests who waited in line. Beyond the glimmering pool, her father had catered a luau. Live Hawaiian music lent a subtle and sensual atmosphere to the night and the perfume of the flowers around her neck made her ache for Zack's touch.

It was clear to her that it wasn't hard for Zack to let her go. She'd taken a risk on Zack and it hadn't panned out. She would have to enjoy the last few days she had with him and then move on to her next competition in Tahiti. By then she hoped she'd still have a sponsor.

She spotted her father near the *imu,* the pit where the pig and sweet potatoes were wrapped in *laulau,* or taro leaves. She could smell the delicious aroma of pork. This particular *imu* had been constructed by digging a hole in the sand and then placing *kiawe* logs in the bottom topped with river rocks. The fire was started and when the hot coals and rocks were ready, moist banana stalks were placed on top followed by a bed of banana leaves on which the pig was placed. The low tables were already set with *poi,* chicken long rice, *lomi* salmon and salads. She was delighted to see that her father hadn't forgotten that *haupia,* or coconut custard, was her favorite dessert.

"Daddy," she called and he looked up from supervising the extraction of the pig and sweet potatoes from the *imu* and waved. He left the caterers to their job and made his way to her across the sand. He threw his arms around her and hugged her so hard, her spine protested. All her doubts seemed to melt away in his exuberance.

"It's good to see you, my girl. I'm happy you came."

"Dad, this is Zack Fanning."

"Fanning. I know you."

"Yes, sir," Zack said, looking every inch the groupie. "I have to warn you that I brought a poster for you to sign."

Her father laughed. "Be happy to. Maybe later we can talk."

"Yes, sir. I'll go get us some drinks, JC."

"Are you still going by that nickname, even to your boyfriends?"

"Dad! Zack isn't my boyfriend."

"Right, sorry. I just like Jade so much better."

"Jade! That's your first name?" Zack exclaimed. "It's beautiful. I want to call you Jade from now on."

"Don't you dare, Zack. See what you've done, Dad."

Her father only chuckled.

"Zack Fanning, huh?" her father said as Zack strolled over to the bar.

"He crashed into me when I was practicing a couple of weeks ago. He broke my board and insisted on making me a new one. In fact, he's made me three."

"I'd like to see them."

"I'll show them to you later. Are you coming to the competition?"

"I wouldn't miss it for the world."

"I thought you might be a little mad."

"No, just wondering why it's taken you so long to come see me."

"I'm having a difficult time, Dad. Lexie told me that if I don't do well in this competition, they're dropping me. My stats are terrible and I thought you'd be...."

"What? Disappointed in you? Ah, honey. I don't care about any of that. You're my daughter, and I love you. I couldn't ever be disappointed in you."

"You must have read what they've said about me."

"What have they said?"

"That I'm not you. That I had so much potential that hasn't been realized."

"Screw them. What do they know? Of course, you're not me. You're Jade Crystal Wilcox and you are your own person, and tomorrow you're going to get your rhythm back and kick ass in the Pipe."

"Damn right," Zack chimed in as he handed her a cocktail. She sipped at the drink and smiled.

"That pig smells mighty good, Slade," a dark-haired man said as he came up to them.

"Evan. It's good to see you."

"Evan Banks?" JC asked, turning to look at Zack.

"Yes, do I know you?"

"Evan, this is my daughter, JC Wilcox and her friend, Zack Fanning."

"Zack Fanning. That's a name I know. I heard good things about you and your boards and designs. My girlfriend's a photographer and she mentioned you might be looking to expand your business."

Zack didn't say anything and JC's heart constricted in her chest.

"I don't know about that, sir," Zack replied.

Evan pulled a card out of his pocket and handed it to Zack. "I'd like to see your plans, young man. Let's set something up. Call me." Evan and her father walked away.

Zack held the business card as if it was a scorpion. "What did you do?"

"I mentioned it to the photographer at the photo shoot," answered JC. "How did I know that she was dating him?"

"You mentioned that I might be interested in expanding my business?"

"No, I said I wished that you'd expand your business. You know how things can get mixed up."

"JC, I told you—"

"I know, and I'm sorry. It just came out. But now that you have his card…"

"I guess it couldn't hurt to talk to the guy. I'm flattered that he would be interested in investing in me."

"Really? That's great. I could put together a marketing plan for you. I majored in marketing in college."

Zack looked at JC and after a moment, nodded. "Okay, but I'm not making any promises."

"Just wait until you see my plan. We'll get that money for you in no time. I've had three women stop me and ask me where I got the halter outfit. One of them offered to buy it when I told her it was one of a kind. This will be big."

The next few hours passed quickly, and the hot afternoon turned into a warm evening. Still, the party continued and JC got full on roasted pig and lots of coconut custard. She was happy and content. Tomorrow she was going to prove to everyone that she had what it took to compete.

She glanced at Zack, who was sitting back and watching her with a light in his eyes. "As much as I hate to leave, I have to get a good night's sleep to be fresh for tomorrow," she told him.

She said her goodbyes to her father and he reassured her that he would be at the competition tomorrow. Once she was seated in Zack's Jeep, Zack threaded his fingers through her hair, cupped the back of her head and pulled her forward so that she was meeting him halfway. Without preamble, he melded her mouth to his, and her lips parted, inviting a deeper, intimate kiss.

He quit kissing her abruptly at the knock on the window. JC burst out laughing when she saw her father's amused face staring at them. Zack hit the quick-release button and the glass slid down. "Yes, sir?" Zack asked.

"I came out because you forgot to get me to sign that poster."

"Right," Zack said, his voice cracking. He reached into the backseat and handed the poster and a marker to her father. She giggled again and Zack gave her a sheepish look as her father signed the poster, "From one wave rider to another, surfing is a way of life. Live it! Slade Wilcox."

Zack took the poster and JC's father made his way over to her side of the car. He bent down to kiss her cheek and said softly, "Not your boyfriend, my ass."

JC burst out laughing again, and as her father walked away,

Zack tugged her close to wheedle out of her what her father had said, but she held firm.

He rested his forehead against hers. The interior of the vehicle was dark, but the air around them fairly crackled with awareness and sexual tension.

"We'd better get a move on. You wouldn't want my father to come back out and…"

"No, I wouldn't." Zack started the engine and drove back to his house. When he parked, his mouth took hers again in a lazy, mindless, tongue-tangling kiss that seemed to go on for long, slow minutes. By the time he let her up for air again, her skin felt flushed, and she was breathing much too fast.

Somehow, she managed to hold on to a rational thought. "I really should make you take me to the bungalow so I get a good night's sleep."

"I'll make it good."

"That's what I'm afraid of."

He took her hand and JC couldn't break away. Didn't want to break away. At this point she wanted to spend every second she could with Zack.

"How about a dip in the hot tub?" he asked.

"Sounds good. I do feel a bit sore from practice, but I don't have my suit."

"You don't need your suit."

"That's completely decadent."

He led her through the house to the back where he flipped some switches. Lights came on in the pool area and in the pool, illuminating the water to a gorgeous teal-green. He flipped more switches and the lights near the hot tub came on and JC heard the soft hum, then thrashing water.

Zack stepped onto the patio and started shucking his clothing, leaving a trail all the way to the hot tub. Her appreciative gaze traveled over his well-defined back and his cute backside before he sank into the water.

She slipped off her sandals and stood on the patio, the concrete warm beneath her feet. The breeze off the ocean was brisk. It lifted her dark hair, sending a cool, caressing breeze across the back of her neck. It felt good.

When she reached the tub, she slid her skirt down her legs and stepped out of it. Pulling off her T-shirt and dropping it onto the concrete along with her skirt, she unsnapped her bra and slipped off her panties.

Zack watched her every move. She tiptoed to the deck and lowered herself down into the tub. "I didn't realize how hot the water would be."

"Let's cool you off," he said as he picked up a spray bottle that he used to cool himself on hot days. He spritzed her just as the wind came up again. She shivered as the first fine droplets of water beaded on her hot, naked skin, both refreshing and arousing her to a higher level of need. At her reaction, he misted his way down her body. An exhilarating draft of air kissed her bared, moist flesh.

Letting her head fall back, she closed her eyes, saturating her mind with the highly electrifying sensations.

"Damn, you make me rock-hard." His voice was low, thick; he sounded devastatingly aroused.

His hands captured her breasts, encircling them, possessive fingers caressed her rigid nipples before he continued on with his lazy journey…skimming his palms across her quivering belly and down to her thighs.

JC moaned at the delightful feel of Zack's hot, questing hands sliding over her slick flesh.

Their eyes met in the shadowed darkness, and there was no mistaking the hard, solid length of his erection jutting against her mound. He rolled his hips, and JC felt his desire for her.

"I like rock-hard," she murmured.

Widening her stance, she arched toward him, silently seeking more. "Oh, yes," she whispered, "I really like rock-hard."

Lowering his head, he kissed her, voracious and hungry, and she answered, grinding her body sensually against his in a rhythm that matched the thrust of his tongue.

One of his hands grasped her gyrating hip, traveling over her bottom to hook his long fingers behind her knee. He lifted her leg up to his waist, wedged his thigh tightly between hers, and pressed his groin to her sex, urging her to feel him, all of him.

Every single hard inch.

She wanted him inside her while the water bubbled around them and the wind blew across their hot, aroused bodies.

His hands encircled her waist and she found herself back on the deck. Her confusion only lasted a moment as he knelt at the tip of the tub, the water churning around his hips. Gliding one finger across her pubic bone made JC gasp. Still kneeling at the edge of the tub, he pushed her legs apart. She moaned and jutted her hips eagerly toward him.

Her sex felt swollen, slick with her own desire. He fondled her pulsing clit, and his tongue circled it with wet flicks, accelerating her heart rate. Then his lips closed over her, and he took her eagerly, hotly, greedily, triggering her strongest orgasm yet.

He pulled her back into the water and pressed her against the side of the tub. The sound that slid from her was raw and guttural as he pushed fully into her. She was ready for him, and pushed back against him, but there was nothing hurried this time. His strokes were slow, controlled and oh so deep, but the connection she felt with him as their gazes held with each thrust was as primeval as it got. She braced her hands on the deck of the tub as he leaned over her, taking her tingling lips, while his hands slid up her torso. He teased her nipples, twisting groan after groan from her, finally drawing a low cry of ecstasy when he slid one hand between her thighs.

She peaked quickly, almost ferociously, and he remained there, his fingers deft and skillful, kept her shaking and gyrating, until he was shuddering with the effort to fend off his own orgasm. She pushed against him again, needing more of him somehow and yet feeling so completely full of him that tears pricked the back of her eyes.

His hands found her hips, his fingers digging in tightly as he began pumping vigorously. She met him thrust for thrust, her hands slipping on the ledge. The connection she felt to him was profound. His climax, when he finally gave in to it, was frantic as he drove into her. Body slapping against body, their cries of pleasure filled the air.

He collapsed over her, and they both sank into the water. He held her tightly to him, his body still shuddering in the aftermath.

Sex in the hot tub was such a fantasy, but this wasn't a fantasy. It had felt like more, a lot more. They had made a connection; she'd seen it in his eyes. Or had she? Was she playing herself for a fool? Most likely. Then she felt him press a kiss to her hair, and her heart swelled. So stupid, so silly, she scolded herself. Mistaking sex for love. For anything other than what it was. Pleasure. Profound in this case, life-altering even, but mere physical gratification nonetheless.

Yet it was much too late for her to pull back and ignore these feelings, and no amount of kicking herself for being a fool was going to change that. It was then she realized how much she'd risked, letting him touch her at all. It wasn't the competition, or anything material that she'd jeopardized. What it was, was irreplaceable. It was her heart. How had she been so naive as to think it was something she could give away and not suffer for her folly in the end?

Independence mocked her and she clenched her hands into fists against Zack's back to keep herself from holding on. She wanted to end their embrace and enjoy the warm, soothing water, tease him about the out-of-control, fabulous sex they experienced every time they got naked, as casual lovers would, as if their lovemaking meant nothing.

He caressed her cheek with the backs of his fingers. Subtly, she turned her head, not wanting him to see what might be in her eyes at that moment. She felt unprepared to face him and vulnerable in a way that had absolutely nothing to do with her nakedness, and everything to do with her emotions. He'd comforted her, and he had an uncanny way of knowing how she felt. Perhaps it was the shared sport and their circumstances, but JC was sure that even if he was unprepared for what he might find, she doubted he'd miss what her eyes revealed.

She didn't want this to end right now. She knew it was selfish, but if she was going to risk being with him, she wanted to enjoy it.

But then, she already knew there wasn't going to be any getting enough where Zack was concerned. More now was only going to hurt more later. Yet she couldn't seem to care.

"Show me those pretty eyes because there's a whole lot going on with you," he said, his voice hardly more than a gravelly rasp.

She had no choice, that soft-toned voice, his compassion, tugged on her heartstrings until she turned her head and looked at him. Stunned, she could only stare into his eyes. Eyes that weren't filled with desire or satisfied pleasure. In those blue, blue depths, she saw an easy, honest affection, so direct, so open, so…naked. Exposed. As exposed as she felt. He peered so far into her, with such blatant need, she didn't know it was possible to be touched so deeply.

Was it wishful thinking? She made herself consider the possibility. But she concluded that it would require a lot of imagination to come up with such a profound, raw intensity.

"I—"

"JC," he said at the same time.

"What?"

"You go," he prompted. His arms banded more tightly around her. When she didn't speak, he said, "Please say something."

Her heart thudded in her chest. She had no expectations of what she would tell him. Certainly not some mushy proof of love. No matter what his eyes said, she could hear trepidation in his voice. Zack's fear would keep them apart even though he wanted something more. She would not try to persuade him. He was the one who had lost so much and although he denied it, he hadn't gotten over it. No amount of fantasy would change what they were even though there was so much potential for what they might want to be.

"I don't know what to say." She started to pull away.

He wouldn't let her go. Instead, he sighed heavily, then pressed his head to hers. "I feel so close to you and I don't want to let you go," he said, the words hardly more than a rasp.

She slipped her fingers into his thick hair, kneading his scalp, her heart responding to his words. She never wanted to let him go, either. "Yeah," she whispered, "I know the feeling."

"It's not the sex," he said. The only sound in the night was the splash and bubble of the water. "But I have to confess I'm hard again just thinking about you."

She started to lift her head, ready to diffuse the tension with a teasing smile and a smart and clever remark. She was prepared to ignore completely the confusion she heard in his voice that so clearly mirrored her own.

But he tightened his arms around her, their gazes, for once, not on each other. Maybe that was the only way he could say what he needed to say, she thought.

She told herself that the fact that he was wrestling with his own emotions was something special. It would have to do. He told her with his touch and his body that she hadn't given her heart in vain. That would have to be enough.

He opened his mouth, but before he could say anything at all, his phone rang. The cell was in his shorts near the patio door. He got out of the water and grabbed the phone. Turning away from her, he started to talk.

It would have to be enough, she thought again sadly. He was still running from the pain and disappointment of life. He might deny it, but she'd seen it before in her own eyes as she looked back at herself in the mirror. Getting out of the tub, she snagged a towel off the deck and wrapped it around her.

She passed him and felt the soft caress of his hand on her arm as she moved by him. She didn't look back.

6

DRIVEN by the storm, the waves of the Pipe roared shoreward. Wisps of red and purple smudged the distant sky, tingeing the rolling water a rich magenta. Crashing onto the sloping beach, the cresting waves warred with the twilight. JC let a handful of powdery white sand sift from her fingers as she stared into the teeth of the storm. Only the toss of spray marred the deepening reddish-purple hue.

She embraced the sense of weightlessness she felt as a child when her father had taught her to float in these waters. The same feeling she achieved each time she mounted a surfboard. She had won the first heat of the Girls Go Banzai competition, and the second, but the approaching storm had caused the waves to become treacherous, so the third heat would have to wait until tomorrow.

They had been there, both Zack and her father, to watch her take the tube as though she'd been born of the waves.

She'd never forget that exhilarating drop or the feeling of just *knowing* that she was riding a wave that was sending her into the third heat on top. Her sponsor had been ecstatic.

Her father had hugged her after she'd come out of the water, the look on his face saying that he couldn't have been prouder.

Zack had kissed her hard in front of everyone.

In the meantime, Evan Banks had convinced Zack to have dinner with him tonight and he'd invited her, as well. But after her shower, she'd just had to come back out here and relive her victory.

After a few more minutes, she got up from the sand. Clutched in her hand was the marketing plan she'd written for Zack. She headed for the restaurant.

ZACK WORKED at the rails of the surfboard. His shoulders felt tight and he tried to shrug off the feeling of losing something that he knew he was never going to find again, but the heaviness in his heart wouldn't lift.

Suddenly his sander stopped and he looked up right into the stormy eyes of JC. She was holding the end of the cord, the plug dangling from her fingers.

"Did you forget about something important tonight?" She accused. She had every right to do so. He was a damned coward and it was time that she knew it.

He set his jaw and looked past her into the dark night. He wanted her. That wasn't the question. The question was whether or not he was willing to risk it. "I'm sorry, but I'm not ready for this."

She dropped the cord and glared at him. "For this? What does that mean?"

He could see that she knew what it meant and she wasn't going to give him an out.

"I'm not ready for my business to grow and for…"

"Me," she said, her voice breaking. "You're not ready for me."

He met her eyes, but glanced away when he saw the pain and regret there. It had hurt so much the last time he'd lost something so important in his life. The answers eluded him, lay inside him beneath a dark cloak he hadn't worked up the courage to look beneath. It was easier not to, simpler to let her walk out of his life. "No. I'm not."

"That's garbage." Her tone snapped with anger and disappointment. "You don't want to move on. You want to live in the past, not in the present. You never even tried to make your dreams into a new reality."

"I can't."

"You disappoint me. You're not the Zack Fanning I once thought I knew."

"You never knew me. That Zack Fanning doesn't exist anymore."

"Yes, he does. He's there. You just have to find him."

"Go back to your competition, surfer girl. You're on top now."

"I'm sure you're happy about that now that I won the first and second heats, aren't you? Now, you won't have to take a risk on me. I'll be moving on."

"There's nothing more to say. We had a good time, you and me. You never had any intention of staying anyway. We both know that. Life has a way of taking over your life."

"To hell with you. You never even asked me to stay."

He was nipping this disaster in the bud. She was going to win this competition and she was going to leave. He couldn't ask her to stay and give up her dreams. She would resent him in the end. He loved her. But this was the best thing he could do for both of them. God, his heart hurt as he watched her walk away.

JC SAT on the sand, waiting for her turn at heat three. The weather had cleared, and it was so clear and beautiful outside, she couldn't wait to get at the waves.

Her encounter with Zack last night after the embarrassing wait with Mr. Banks at the restaurant was fresh in her mind. If she had any sense at all, she would forget about Zack Fanning, a man much too afraid of grasping the future because he was holding on to the past so tightly. He was forever caught in a terrible limbo. Though he'd taught her something vital, something she might have never learned otherwise. Her dreams didn't have to be static and old. JC could reinvent them any way she chose. She wished she could have taught Zack that, as well.

JC closed her eyes and turned her face up to the sun. She let herself picture a life where they could truly start over, where people really did rise above their pasts and lived beyond the shadows. A place where she and Zack could simply have happiness without all the baggage attached.

"JC."

It took a moment for JC to recognize the voice. Her eyes flew open, and she swung around in the sand to see Zack. He was dressed in a white T-shirt that accentuated his tan and a pair of denim cutoffs that made her throat tighten with the memories. Lines of strain were etched around his impossibly blue eyes. He smiled his enticing smile, but there was too much pain in his expression for him to quite pull it off.

"What are you doing here?" she asked, standing.

He reached out his hand and offered her a sheaf of papers.

"What are these?" She took them and immediately saw it was a contract. He'd gone through with the deal with Evan Banks and a frisson of hope blossomed in her.

"Good for you. I'm happy for you," she said as she handed the papers back to him. She had to turn away, not quite ready to put her heart on the line again.

"Don't go." His voice was barely a whisper above the waves.

JC froze, but then she turned back and took a step toward him.

He continued, his voice subdued, his eyes pleading and vulnerable. "I didn't ask before because…how could I ask you to give up your dream? I lost mine, but I never let it go. I let the rage and resentment close me off to taking any kind of risk. I was afraid of failing again, so it was better not to take the chance at all."

"What changed your mind?"

"You did. I watched you get out there and battle like a champion. Your courage shamed me, made me finally face my fear. That's when I contacted Evan Banks and made the deal. That's why I'm here to tell you…"

"What?"

"I'm in love with you and I don't want you to leave. I understand you'll have commitments on the circuit, but let this be your home base." He sounded so earnest. The wind blew his thick blond hair across his forehead. "Let me be your home base."

She threw herself into his arms and hung on. She pressed her cheek against his chest. "You taught me something, too, Zack."

"I can't imagine what."

"You taught me that dreams can change. I've made a decision. I'm quitting after this competition. I've already made up my mind. Win or lose. It's time for me to retire and let the sweet young things have a turn. I've had such a great career just like you said. There are so many other things I want to do. Hell, I can always surf. It's been such an important part of my whole life. My dad's here, too. I want to be close to him, maybe even help out with his surfing camp."

"Are you sure about that?"

"Yes, I'm sure. It opens up a whole new world of possibilities." At Zack's speculative look, JC said, "You have something in mind?"

"How about you put that marketing degree to use and work with me?"

"I like the way you said that. *Work with you.* Sounds like a great plan to me." She picked up her board just as her name was called for the heat. Walking to the surf, she stopped suddenly and turned around. "I love you, too, Zack, in case you weren't sure about that."

He bridged the distance. "I was hoping. Go knock 'em dead, tiger."

"I will."

JC paddled into the surf and watched the huge waves roll by. Sure, she'd won the first two heats, and she knew now that it didn't matter if she won this final one or not. Her heart was already the real winner.

In fact, she and Zack were the very luckiest winners of all.

* * * * *

WET AND WILD
Jill Monroe

This book is dedicated to my family. Thank you for your support. Pink, I love you!

A special thanks to Karen Anders and Julie Kenner. This was fun to write with the two of you!

I'd also like to thank my agent, Deidre Knight—
I so appreciate you—and Kathryn Lye, who finds all my repetitive and awkward sentences and makes them better.

No dedication would be complete without thanking Jennifer, Kassia, Karen and Maggie—such great friends—and of course Gena Showalter. A very difficult person to interview!

1

"I PROMISE I'll be good," Andrea "Drea" Powell told Kaydee as their feet sank into the warm sand of the beach. The ocean beckoned a few yards away. The waves were breaking perfectly and Drea couldn't wait to paddle out and ride them. She gripped her board tighter as they walked toward the water's edge. The waves off Oahu were legend, and right now with their high swells and consistent sets, they were living up to their reputation.

Kaydee gasped then shook her head. "You couldn't even be convincing when you told me that. It's pathetic."

Drea made a face. "I just don't know why I can't be myself to get the sponsorship."

"You *are* being yourself. We're only changing your personality. The rest is all you," her friend said with a wink.

"Thanks a lot," Drea said, as she kicked sand over Kaydee's toes.

Kaydee's expression grew serious. "Listen, bottom line is, no matter how good a surfer you are, no company is going to sink one dime on you if they think you're going to bolt at any minute. Or die out there because you took one risk too many."

Drea made a scoffing sound. "They don't give Rookie of the Year to surfers who stay back and play it safe."

Kaydee propped up her board and faced Drea. "Hey, reining in your burning desire for danger will be good for you."

"And my desperate need to prove that winning Rookie of the Year wasn't a fluke," Drea added. "As long as my motivations are being dissected, let's go for the whole deal." This wasn't the first time her friend had brought up these points.

Kaydee braced her hand on her hip. "Okay, then, since you

issued the invitation, I'm going to say it all. Enjoy. Winning the last competition may have given you the money to get to Hawaii and enter Banzai, but what if you don't win here? You'll be working at the Trading Post selling postcards to tourists while the other surfers are packing to go to the next competition. You can't surf and improve if you're counting on wins to get the money. You have to get a sponsorship. It's your insurance in case you don't win. And to get a sponsorship you have to—"

"I have to take it easier," Drea finished for her.

"Some waves aren't meant to be surfed, and I'd like to keep my friend alive for as long as possible."

"Oh, yeah?" Drea asked, feeling uncomfortable with the seriousness of Kaydee's tone. Drea liked everything in her life upbeat and happy. Hmm, she was more like her mom than she'd ever realized. It wasn't just the brown eyes that they shared. Her mom had also gone from one low-paying job to another to support her dream of singing. Same lifestyle…just different dreams.

"Of course. How else am I going to pass my marketing class if I don't have you for a case study?"

There, that's more like it. Light and funny. "Come on, let's hit the beach."

Right. With only two weeks before the competition, she needed as much time in the water as she could get. Drea pivoted toward the surf and…

There he was.

"Look at his style. His control," Drea said with awe about the tall man riding a wave with ease.

"Makes a girl wonder if he loses that control in bed."

Drea glanced sharply at her friend. Did Kaydee know Drea's thoughts often wandered in that direction?

"Come on, it's not like you haven't thought about what Kirk Murray would be like in bed a hundred times."

Try a thousand times.

She and Kaydee simply stood there and watched as the gorgeous man surfed the way surfing was meant to be done. His athleticism was clear, from the muscled strength of his legs, to the ease with which he dipped his fingers into the water.

"There you are, Drea."

Drea reluctantly took her gaze away from Kirk to see Linda coming up beside her.

"I should have known you'd be on the beach," said the friendly and now breathless brunette. Linda was second in command to Taylor Dutton with the Girls Go Banzai surfing competition. "Those waves are pumping."

Drea's fingers tightened around her board. "I can't wait to get out there."

"Well, wait until you hear this. I can't believe it, Drea. You are so lucky," Linda gushed, her tone sounding impressed.

No one could help smiling at Linda. She had the kind of enthusiasm and excitement that was almost catching. Almost.

"What's up?" Drea asked.

"I just heard Kirk Murray wants to meet with you about a full sponsorship."

Drea's stomach lurched at the mention of his name. Anyone's would. Her gaze returned to the sea. Kirk was already paddling out to catch the next wave. As a three-time Longboard World Champion, Kirk had made millions through his endorsements. A true professional surfer, he'd traveled the world and now made frequent appearances on sports TV channels. She'd heard rumors of his retirement—that he wanted to stay put on Oahu and devote more attention to his very popular restaurant, Da Kine.

But sponsorship? Of her? Her heart began to race.

"Yes, she'll take it," Kaydee blurted.

"As if there was any question," Linda scoffed, and the two of them both laughed.

But Drea didn't laugh. Obviously this was the best break she'd gotten outside of the ocean, but Kirk Murray was a man in a different league. She'd talked to him once, two weeks ago. She'd finally scrounged up enough money waiting tables and from selling her bike to fly her and her board from California to Hawaii. As she was filling out the paperwork to make her an official competitor with the Girls Go Banzai surfing competition, the man, literally out of her dreams, walked past.

Never one to pass up an opportunity, she'd said hi. He'd flashed her that fantastic smile of his that graced everything from surf fan posters to ads for board leashes. She started to stutter out something, but then his cell phone rang, and her chance was lost.

Not this time.

"He wants you to meet him at his restaurant at two. Let me give you directions."

But Drea didn't need them. She knew exactly where Kirk spent the majority of his time outside of the water. Had walked by it three times.

"Okay, gotta run. So many last-minute details," Linda said and continued down the beach.

"This is it for you. I can feel it," Kaydee said once Linda was out of earshot.

"If you thought my promise to be good was pathetic, remember how I was around him?"

Kaydee ran her finger through her hair. "Um, actually, I was embarrassed for you."

Drea grimaced.

"Oops, sorry. I'm supposed to be more supportive than that."

"Forget it, you were just telling the truth."

"Sometimes the truth shouldn't be told."

"Said like someone who plans to make a career out of marketing."

Kaydee smiled. "Let me try this again. Really, I'm a much better friend. Supportive even."

Drea laughed, then pretended to brace herself. "Fine, I'm ready."

"The last time you met Kirk Murray you were just an unknown surfer bumming her way from one beach to another. You're the celebrated Rookie of the Year now. And why is that? Because you're good and now you have the cred to back it up. Don't forget *he's* interested in *you*." Kaydee gave a gentle squeeze to Drea's shoulder. "Now is your chance to really show him what you can do."

Drea raised an eyebrow. "I'm really impressed. That was downright inspirational."

"Did you believe it?"

"No, but the hand thing you did was a nice touch."

"Wait, I want you to completely forget that if you impress this man, you could get the kind of sponsorship that would allow you to quit selling seashell necklaces, waitressing or whatever job you can find to support your sport and be on the competitive surf circuit full-time. All your dreams would finally become real."

Drea sucked in a quick breath. "Technically, that was worse."

"How about, 'put your big-girl bikini bottoms on and stop acting like an angsty teen with her first crush.'"

"Your skills at motivation leave me speechless."

"So what are you going to wear?"

Drea's eyes widened. She hadn't thought of that.

"Come on, Drea. Flip-flops, shorts and a hoodie isn't really dressing to impress."

"The only other option is a bikini. I don't have the proper clothes for a job interview." She never had. The muscles in her stomach started to tighten. She also didn't have any experience with the business side of surfing, and knew zilch about how people behaved. Did they shake hands? Dear Lord...heels?

"Don't worry about it, I'll loan you a sundress." Kaydee picked up her board. "Come on, we'll surf away those nerves."

KIRK DRAPED his towel around his neck and peered out to the ocean one last time. The waves were breaking beautifully, and he could easily have surfed another hour without getting tired. Longer periods in the ocean helped with his physical conditioning, and his pop-up was getting sloppy, a bad habit he was determined to change.

He'd love nothing better than to paddle back out, but his day was booked with meetings. He slicked his hand down his face, removing the last traces of the salty water. Meetings, paperwork and corporate networking weren't what he'd had in mind when he realized he needed plans for when he fully retired from the professional surfing circuit. No, all that serious stuff sounded a bit too much like his dad. Kirk's idea of retirement was catching waves in the morning, playing on the beach with his nephew and spending his evenings in Da Kine, the restaurant he'd started two years ago.

Too bad his ideas and reality weren't meshing. But he'd get there. Just like with his surfing, if he put in the hard work, it would all pay off.

He was just about to reach for his board and head for the car, when the bright flash of a red bikini in the blue of the water caught his eye. Mesmerized, he watched as the surfer angled and turned, making one brash move and taking one risk after another out there in the water. He'd be horrified if he weren't utterly captivated. Just like every other man out on the beach, he noted.

"There are days when I think I'm a pretty good surfer. Then I see her, and I feel like a grommet."

Kirk tore his gaze away from the beauty in the ocean to see Taylor Dutton's second in command staring wistfully out into the water. "You're not a grommet," he told her. The term was used for young surfers.

"Thanks, Kirk," she said, smiling.

"You're too old to be a grommet."

"Whatever," Linda said as she gave him a playful jab in the ribs. "By the way, she's confirmed for two. She'll meet you at the restaurant."

His gaze returned to the woman who'd just jumped off her board and into the ocean. No smooth glide into the water at the end of her run. His muscles tensed as he waited for her to resurface. Then he saw her head pop out of the water and he could breathe again. She was paddling back out to the breaking waves when he realized Linda's meaning. "That's Andrea Powell? The woman you suggested I sponsor?"

Linda nodded.

"Are you kidding? Look at her. She's like a wild thing out there."

"Which makes her all the better match for you. You said you wanted someone who you could help train, give pointers to. You have to admit she's got the guts, it's her style she needs to work on."

The woman took on the wave like she was challenging it to knock her off the board. He admired her determination.

"And catch the attention she's already getting in and out of the water. The other surfers are getting out of her way."

"That's not necessarily a good thing," he said drily.

"Then look at the beach. What she has grabs people's interest, and that is a win-win when it comes to sponsorship."

Linda had a point. Which was probably why she was so valuable to Taylor Dutton.

"She does look fearless," he said. And sexy.

"I knew this would work," Linda said with a laugh. "I can already hear the excitement in your voice."

"All she needs is a little technique and a little more discipline. She could be number one on the circuit in no time."

"And she can do it all while wearing a Da Kine shirt or bathing suit. No one will forget her or your restaurant. Like I said, it's win-win."

Linda was very right. He couldn't stop his eyes from drifting over the curves of the woman mastering the waves. The Pipeline was a monster, and she was handling it with skill and amazing beauty. He smiled, and his reluctance to leave the beach vanished. In just a few hours, he'd have that beauty to himself.

When he woke up this morning, the day that stretched before him meant practice time at the ocean and then a series of meetings. Now he was looking forward to two o'clock in a way he hadn't looked forward to something in a long while.

"Win-win for sure."

AN HOUR before she was supposed to meet with Kirk Murray, Drea had convinced herself that someone was playing a joke on her. No way would the great Kirk Murray actually be interested in sponsoring her. The man was a legend and he wasn't even thirty.

Someone must have discovered the secret crush and set her up. She was an outsider, and certainly didn't fit with the close-knit group of surfers. But who would be that cruel? JC and Laci were her biggest competitors, but neither seemed the type.

Besides, they'd become such good friends while sharing their rented bungalow during this competition.

Maybe it was true. Maybe Kirk Murray really did want to sponsor her. A sponsorship would mean so much to her. She could get off her diet of whatever food the restaurant where she worked didn't want. She could be on the surfing circuit from Florida to Australia, Fiji, wherever, and not have to sell off her possessions or plasma. She could make something of herself.

She sucked in a deep breath and held it, willing her nerves to settle down. She'd surfed the Pipeline, practiced in the shark-infested waters around Florida and sold absolutely everything she owned but her board to compete. But she'd never been this nervous.

She'd fallen for Kirk hard-core the first time she'd spotted him surfing in a competition in California. New to the sport herself, and supporting herself waitressing, there was no way she could afford lessons. She learned by trial and error, and what she couldn't figure out on her own, she did by observing the surfers in the water. No one was a better teacher than Kirk Murray. His style and form were about as perfect as a surfer could get.

If she hadn't already admired him for his surfing skills, seeing the man up close and personal had sealed the deal. He was tall and lean, his muscles stretched across his chest, showing his strength. He wore his dark blond hair short and spiky in a way that just made her want to mess it up. His green eyes surveyed the water so intently; she knew he was reading the ocean, learning the wave pattern so he could catch the best one. She wanted to be able to do that. She wanted him to teach her. And then she wanted him to look at her just as intently. To want to read and learn all the things about her, the way she did about him.

And she did know almost everything about him. After seeing him surf in California, she'd found a few moments alone on the Internet at the public library and searched every article that mentioned his name.

Single—yes.

Owned a restaurant—yeah, they had something in common. She'd worked in plenty.

Home base—Hawaii. And that was why she was here in Oahu at the Girls Go Banzai competition instead of staying in California and building her reputation in a place that was already familiar.

When she'd explained to Kaydee how she made it to Hawaii, the woman had thought she was crazy. But she'd lived her life flying by the seat of her pants and not taking the safe way, and she wasn't going to change now. Those very traits had won her the Rookie of the Year award and now, very possibly, a sponsorship with Kirk Murray and an opportunity to spend a lot of one-on-one time with the man himself.

She smoothed the skirt of the sundress Kaydee had loaned her, took a deep breath and reached for the door handle of Da Kine.

2

DREA HAD DROPPED blue-plate specials, spilled drinks and brought the wrong food to plenty of customers in the dozens of restaurants she'd been fired from, but none of them had possessed the warmth and welcome of Kirk's Da Kine. Donning an apron and closed-toe rubber-soled shoes might not even be a chore here. Journalists, surfers and fans all mingled together.

If the noise level was any indication, the patrons enjoyed the place as much as she suspected she would. Laughter was abundant, as was the surf paraphernalia, which wasn't surprising, seeing as Kirk had named his restaurant for the Hawaiian phrase for the best kind of wave. She expected to see more pictures of him; after all, that body could probably sell a lot of hamburgers and exotic martinis.

The broken board he'd ridden when he won his first championship was mounted high on the wall. Framed jerseys and wetsuits dotted the walls. Da Kine made her think of traditional Hawaii, minus the expected tourist tackiness. The shades of blues expressed a love of the ocean, and the traditional fare showed a love of the culture.

And Drea felt completely out of place in her borrowed green sundress and unpainted toenails. She eyed the door, ready to bolt.

"Drea."

A shiver ran down her back. She'd recognize that sexy, commanding voice above the din of a crowded restaurant or the roar and splash of the ocean. Drea had heard it often enough in television interviews and the homemade surf videos people uploaded on the Internet.

Kirk Murray.

She turned at the sound of her name and her breath hitched when she saw him. He was even better-looking up close and personal. No camera did justice to his deep green eyes, or showed the true friendliness in his smile. Wearing khaki shorts and a blue polo shirt, he looked just as good out of the water as he did wearing nothing but his swim trunks.

Well, almost. Without his shirt, he was beautiful.

"Hi, I'm Kirk," he said as he stretched out a hand. "So glad you could make it."

Good Lord, she'd have to touch him. Get to touch him. Drea stuck out her own hand, and his engulfed hers. How Kirk made her feel warm and welcome with such a simple gesture, which people did every day, she'd never know, but he did, and her nerves vanished.

"Hungry?" he asked. "The grill is up and running."

For the first time she noticed the inviting scents of roasted pineapple, banana bread and seafood. She'd had a peanut butter and jelly sandwich before she'd left Kaydee's apartment with the sundress, so unfortunately she was full.

She shook her head. "Already ate."

"Then how about a walk on the beach? One of the perks of owning a place so close. That way we can get to know each other better."

That sounded more like employment Q&A, and her nerves kicked up again. "I'd like that."

He opened the door for her, and she blinked against the brightness of the sun before sliding her sunglasses down her nose.

"So tell me about yourself. The information Linda gave me left a lot of blanks," he said once they'd deposited their shoes in the bin provided by Da Kine and their feet were firmly in the sun-warmed sand.

"I like a lot of blanks."

He smiled. "You're one of those."

She glanced up. One of the great things about surfing was that it was a sport that didn't require a participant to be tall. At five foot five, Drea was comfortable with her average height, but she had to look up, very up, for her gaze to meet Kirk's green eyes. "One of those—?"

"The kind of person that any answer has to be dragged out of them."

He had her pegged. Drea didn't like talking about herself, not because she had some big, dark secret lurking, there just weren't a lot of interesting things to tell. Surfing and waiting tables to pay for her surfing was pretty much her life. "Actually, I'm an open book. Ask me anything," she invited with a teasing smile.

"Where are you from?"

"All over."

"Originally," he said with a laugh.

"Springfield, Missouri."

"Landlocked. How'd you end up surfing?" he asked as people milled slowly around them. The pace here in Hawaii was slower, more laid-back than even California. She was used to a more frenetic lifestyle.

"My mom had what she called restless feet. All she ever wanted to do was write songs and play them on her guitar in front of a crowd. We never stayed in one place for very long. Then we ended up in Florida. She had a job waitressing in Seaside, and one day I saw someone surfing."

A slow smile appeared on his face, and he stopped walking. "And you were hooked."

"Yeah." She liked this. Drea actually liked this. The way she'd grown up, and her current nomadic lifestyle never offered much opportunity to connect with others. But Kirk's tone and expression told her he understood *exactly* what she *felt,* how she felt the first time she saw someone surf. The first time she stood on a board and rode a wave. The first time she wiped out.

A warm breeze came from the ocean, blowing through the sun-bleached tips of his hair. She sensed he was studying her face. Thankfully she was wearing her sunglasses. She'd had a crush on this man for two years, but none of that was real. This moment was real. *He* was real, and she was afraid her eyes would show just how important this meeting was to her, professionally and personally.

Kirk turned his head and began walking up the beach again. "Who'd you take lessons from? I know some trainers based out of Florida."

A question she hadn't expected. Would he still take her seriously when he learned the answer? "I never took lessons."

"How'd you learn?" he asked, surprise lacing his voice.

"Self-taught mostly. I watched some videos on the Internet and checked books out of the library."

"I'm still just amazed anytime I run into someone who's out there winning competitions and didn't even have a coach."

"If I fell off my board, I tried to figure out why, and then not do that anymore."

Kirk laughed. "That philosophy would have saved my dad thousands of dollars."

Drea joined him, enjoying the deep rumble of his laughter. She knew from Kirk's bio that his rich hotel-owning father had shelled out all kinds of cash to get his son the best instruction around. Of course, Kirk had the drive and the skill to back it up, but there were certainly no hot-dog-only days in Kirk's life as there were for a lot of the surfers on the circuit. Like her.

"The information Linda provided said you won Rookie of the Year out of California. How long did you stay in Florida?" he asked as he continued to walk down the beach. Their shoulders were only inches away from each other.

"Two years. Mostly Cocoa Beach and Daytona."

Kirk shuddered. "Sharks."

So the big strong man had a thing about sharks. Okay, very smart, but still...kind of cute.

"That just makes it more fun," she said, smiling.

"Okay, now I read you. You're a thrill-seeker. You live for danger. That explains your surfing."

"What about my surfing?" she asked, feeling a little defensive.

"The way you surf, it's as though you're daring the wave to

throw you off the board. You do realize surfing is not a contact sport?"

"The way I do it it is."

Kirk stopped and he faced her. "No, no no. Surfing is all about becoming one with the water. An extension of the wave, even."

She kept her mouth shut and worked hard at making sure her features didn't show him she clearly thought he was wrong.

"I can see you don't believe me," he said.

Guess she wasn't doing such a good job.

"Tomorrow," he announced, "you, me and our boards are hitting the water. I'm going to show you how to really surf."

She couldn't help the big smile spreading across her face. "Does that mean you're taking me on? I've got the sponsorship?"

His eyes narrowed as if he were still considering it. "We'll see how well you take instruction, but I won't keep you waiting. I'll tell you right after we're done."

She squelched the disappointment she felt at not being offered his sponsorship right away. Had she really expected it so soon?

"Eleven work for you?" he asked.

"I'm on dawn patrol," she told him. The phrase used by people who had to surf early because they'd be at jobs at times like eleven in the morning.

He nodded as if he understood, but she doubted this man had much necessity to be on the beach that early. "Okay, sunrise it is."

THE NEXT MORNING, Drea yawned as she was going through her series of stretches on the beach. She'd hardly slept the night before. One moment she'd been in a deep sleep, the next, awake, excited and nervous. All due to the sexy, intriguing man she'd be meeting up with in just a few hours. To surf with a world champion like Kirk Murray…

Even if he didn't decide to sponsor her, to get pointers from someone so skilled was an unbelievable opportunity.

But it was the prospect of talking and laughing and spending time with a man she admired, found so sexy and wanted to know more about that had given her sleep schedule such fits. Sometimes when a person met a crush, they were disappointed, but Kirk Murray was very crush-worthy.

She felt a tiny prickle of awareness between her shoulder blades. She smiled, knowing Kirk Murray had to be responsible.

"Even in this dim light, I'd be able to spot you with that yellow bikini."

Kirk carried his board with ease, looking pretty good himself this early in the morning in blue swim trunks and with a bright orange-and-red beach towel draped casually around his neck.

"No one can claim they didn't see me coming with this suit," she said.

"Drea, you'd be hard to miss in anything you were wearing."

Was that...? Could that have been...? Had Kirk Murray just flirted with her? Goose bumps formed on her arms at the prospect.

"You paddle out. I want to watch you catch a few waves first."

With a nod, Drea grabbed her board and ran out into the water. She couldn't wait, longing for that first surprising splash of the ocean against her skin. Everything seemed right when she was in the ocean. She never felt awkward, and she knew what she was doing. The waves weren't too high this morning, but good enough to show Kirk what she could do.

She took on the waves, aggressively and fast, quickly getting into her rhythm.

After two runs, Kirk whistled and she returned to shore.

She paddled back, and when her feet could touch, she lifted her board from the water and walked the rest of the way toward the man waiting for her. His expression didn't tell her anything, but gone was the teasing, easygoing guy from the day before. This morning he was all business.

"Drea, when you started your set, you just picked up your board and hit the water."

She nodded. "Right." What was the problem?

"You can't do that in competition. You didn't even take a moment to observe the sets," he told her, referring to the way waves broke into a pattern.

"What's the point? I just paddle out and push through."

"Yes, but you're going to end up wasting a lot of your energy just paddling out. You can maximize your time in the water hitting waves and impressing the judges if you slow down and take a little time. Do some observation. Count the waves in the set and go before the next set starts. If you plan it right, you can diminish the water resistance."

"That makes a lot of sense," she said, nodding.

"Drea, tell me why you're drawn to surfing."

The question came so out of the blue that she answered him honestly without hiding her need to soften her desires. "I live for that rush of adrenaline. That moment right before I pop up on my board to the feel of the water rushing against my bare skin." Her fingers curled around her board. Describing her feelings to Kirk made her want to catch a wave and experience what she'd just expressed even more. "You know, the ancient Islanders surfed naked."

Kirk nodded toward the water. "Feel free."

She laughed. "Maybe another time. How about you? Why do you surf? I feel like you were looking for something in my answer."

"I was, sort of. I surf because it makes me feel like I'm part of something bigger than myself. Out there, alone on my board surrounded by the ocean, I feel at one with nature."

Yeah, no. She didn't feel any of that. She'd met a lot of Zen-type surfers, but had never figured Kirk for one of them. Interesting.

"Come on, surf with me," he said, his voice soft and inviting.

If he'd said, "Come on, let's get a root canal," in that same quiet tone he'd used just now, she probably would have offered to look up the dentist's number in the phonebook. She couldn't imagine anything better than riding the waves with him at her side.

They picked up their boards and walked together toward the water. About twenty feet inside from where the waves were breaking, Kirk sat on his board and glanced her way. "Forget what you know about speed and aggression. Instead, I want you to think about merging with the wave."

Ahh, making her see surfing his way was what he was after. Okay, she could play along, especially if it would get her that sponsorship. Rather than launch herself toward the wave, she slid from her prone position and began to paddle.

"Match your speed to the wave," he called. She glanced over, and he was right beside her. Drea felt the water against her skin, sensed the wave pattern through her board and adjusted her paddling.

"Now let the wave catch you."

This must be the oneness with the water Kirk was talking about earlier. Sure enough, the wave caught her board and began to accelerate. She popped up and began to ride.

She glanced over and saw Kirk surfing beside her. He flashed her a big smile. She'd never actually surfed with another person before. Oh, there'd been plenty of people in the water surfing next to her, but to actually surf with someone was a different experience.

They rode to shore, angling to extend the time of their ride.

"What did you think?" Kirk asked when they were waist-deep in the water.

"That was amazing," she cried. If there were ever words she wished she could call back, it would be those. It would be obvious to a three-year-old she meant the ride with him was amazing, and not the technique of becoming one with the ocean.

The smile faded from his lips, his eyes. "Yes, it was."

He didn't hide the fact that his gaze searched her face, traveled down her body. Focused on her eyes. She knew when she spotted interest in a man's expression. His body stance. Kirk was interested in her for more than business purposes.

Her whole life she'd been a risk-taker. Everything she had was because she went after it. Right now she wanted Kirk. She pushed her board out of her way, stretched on her tiptoes and reached for the back of Kirk's head, drawing his lips down to hers.

3

THE SALTY WATER of the ocean had cooled on his mouth, but his lips were deliciously warm. She closed her eyes and pressed herself against the strong, solid length of his body. For a moment he stood still. Stood still long enough for her almost to pull away. Then, with a groan, his arms wrapped around her hips and he pulled her closer to his chest.

Adrenaline rushed through her, and it had nothing to do with the beach or a wave. It was all about this man.

He wanted her.

Just like she wanted him.

Her nipples tightened beneath her bikini top and her thighs brushed against the roughness of his. His fingers made lazy patterns against the small of her back, which made her want to arch against him.

A catcall came from the beach, and they broke apart.

Kirk scrubbed his hand down his face. "One of my biggest pet peeves is people who make out in public, and here I am doing it myself."

She saw the frustration in his stance. His shoulders were tight, the muscles along his back taut. He hadn't wanted their kiss to end, and even though she was just as disappointed, she was also thrilled that he'd felt the same way.

He shrugged, then flashed her an almost chagrined expression. "Lost my discipline there. Won't happen again."

Like the ocean, like a giant wave, the words that had just come out of Kirk's mouth sounded a lot like a dare. She wanted to make him need to kiss her again and again.

"So you're a man all about control?"

He nodded. "It's what the sport is about."

"No, no. It's not control. It's chaos," she said with an excited smile.

"It's focus."

"Courage and daring."

He shook his head, but a smile tweaked at the corner of his lip. "Discipline. Something you need to become better acquainted with."

Drea raised a brow. "You going to teach me discipline, Kirk?"

"Now that one I'm not even going to touch." Kirk angled his head toward the waves. "Got time for another run?"

That sounded more like what she had in mind. Maybe he was already beginning to see things her way.

Drea looked up at the sun, the poor gal's clock. Disappointment coursed through as she realized the sun was almost directly overhead. "No, I have to get to work."

His eyebrows shot up. "You're working while in training?"

"The winnings from Rookie of the Year only covered my airfare to Hawaii. Luckily, my job at the Trading Post covers my share of the rent." Money. It all came down to money. With her nomadic lifestyle, her mother had raised her not to value it. Of course, that was not really practical when you were trying to buy things like food.

"Okay, let's process what we've done here today," he said, his tone all business.

"The kiss?"

"No, your run."

"Is this what it's like to have a coach?" she asked, as they waded up to the shore.

"I'm taking it easy on you today since you're self-taught. Tomorrow we start early. Wear a bright suit, like you did today."

"How come?" she asked as she headed toward the showers to rinse off.

"My assistant is bringing the video camera so we can film your runs and analyze them later."

"You're kidding. Like what football players do?"

"Exactly."

Drea thrust her board and beach towel to Kirk and stepped under the spray. No matter how much she prepared herself, the blast of cool fresh water was always a shock to her skin. "Yow."

She maneuvered beneath the shower, cold water sluicing down her arms and legs, as she ran her fingers through her hair.

"And to think I was going to take a few more runs and miss this," he said, his voice deep and filled with desire.

Heat warmed her cheeks. She hadn't meant to be provocative. She'd never acted coy or coquettish in her entire life, but having a man that she'd just kissed watch her shower seemed personal. Intimate. A tension zapped between them now. If they were alone, she'd tug him beneath the spray and run her fingers down his chest. His back. Sink her fingers into his hair and explore the texture. Then she'd kiss him until his skin no longer tasted of salt, but of fresh water and sexy man.

Her nipples tightened, and she only hoped if Kirk noticed he'd chalk it up to the cold water and not her naughty thoughts and what she wanted to do to his body.

When she was satisfied most of the salt was out of her hair and off her skin, she reached for her towel. But Kirk draped it over her shoulders, his fingers lightly caressing her arms as his hands fell away.

Now it was his turn, and Drea couldn't wait to watch the water slide down his back and roll along the lines of his muscles. She swallowed, and willed her voice to sound normal. "I'll hold your gear while you rinse off."

Kirk shook his head. "I shower at home."

Now that was a shame. "That's right. You have nowhere else to be until later."

Ahhh, the luxury. That's what having a sponsorship would do for her.

He picked up both their boards. "Come on, I'll walk you to your car. So how'd you do the first time you surfed Pipe?" The Pipeline of the North Shore of Oahu was known for having some of the heaviest, most dangerous breaks in the world.

Drea laughed. "Basically a sand facial. I completely wiped out."

They approached Kaydee's blue Focus and Kirk secured her board to the rack. "Thanks, Kirk. Even if I don't get Da Kine's sponsorship, I want you to know I appreciated the pointers and your time today."

"I know I said I wouldn't keep you waiting, but there are a few details that need to be hammered out."

She nodded. "Right. Sure, I understand," she said, trying to sound blasé. Was he blowing her off?

"That kiss changed things."

Her breath hitched. Had she ruined everything with her impulsive action? She could smack herself. Of course sponsors didn't kiss their promotees.

He nodded back. "And we'll still work on your training tomorrow."

Relief poured through her. She hadn't blown everything. A minute passed without either one of them saying anything.

Okay, this was getting awkward. She needed to change, and he wasn't leaving. She looked at the black asphalt then met his green gaze. "Well, bye then."

"I was going to see you inside your car."

If this weren't such an uncomfortable moment, her heart would probably be doing some kind of melting scenario at his…she didn't even have a word for what he was doing. Gentlemanly behavior?

She wasn't one to be shy, and she wasn't going to start now. "Actually, I was going to change out of my suit."

His brows drew together. "In your car?" he asked, his voice incredulous.

"Of course, haven't you ever done the surfer's change?"

"No. Why can't you just change where you work?"

"A friend of mine got me that job, but the owner of the Trading Post doesn't like surfers. Thinks we're too transient, which is probably true. Something about we're just learning how to use the cash register correctly and then we're out of there chasing a wave somewhere else. Don't worry about me, I've had plenty of practice."

"I'll stand guard to make sure no one sees."

With a roll of her eyes, she opened the car door and draped her long beach towel over the door and to the roof. She secured it in place with the beach bag she'd kept locked in the car. Then she crouched on the seat, and began to strip. She'd changed like this dozens of times, but just like taking the shower, taking off her clothes with Kirk's back to her felt like nothing that should be done on the side of the road.

She had to lighten up the situation.

"I can't believe you've never changed like this. You talk to me about tradition of the sport, but this, my friend, is a time-honored practice that you've completely missed out on." She hooked her fingers around her bikini bottoms and lifted her hips off the seat, sliding the material down her legs.

"Imagining what you're doing right now is driving me crazy."

"Good," she said, not being able to stop her goofy grin. So he planned to keep up with her training, did his statement tell her he planned to kiss her again, too? Her top followed, and she quickly donned her panties and bra. Thank goodness the Post provided free uniforms. She slid the khaki pants up her legs and snapped the Hawaiian-print blouse closed.

She stood and slid back into her flip-flops. "You can look now."

Kirk turned and eyed her new clothing. "Pretty impressive."

She shrugged and reached for a clip out of the bag still keeping the towel in place. With a few quick twists of her wrist, she had her hair firmly secured to the Trading Post's dress code standards.

His gaze lowered to her lips, and she held her breath, wondering if he was going to kiss her this time. Instead, he took a step away from her, lifting his board from where it balanced against Kaydee's car.

With a little wave, she retrieved her beach bag and towel and tossed them into the passenger seat. She started the car, signaled and pulled into traffic.

Drea made a vow that she wouldn't look in the rearview mirror to see if Kirk was where she left him.

She even kept that vow for a good ten yards. Then she looked.
And a tiny thrill ran down her back.

He was watching her drive away.

KIRK WALKED slowly down the beach and toward his own
vehicle. He'd had the best intentions when he'd come up with
the idea of the sponsorship and asked Linda for a few names.

He'd had it lucky, he knew it. His father was one of the most
successful hoteliers on the island and he'd never had to scrimp
and save and sell his belongings the way so many surfers had just
to participate in the sport they loved.

The way Drea had to.

What he hadn't expected was to be completely and totally attracted to Linda's first suggestion, but attracted he was. He'd asked
Taylor's second in command to describe the sponsorship prospect,
but Linda's cryptic "brown hair, brown eyes and average height"
hadn't prepared him for the beat-down Drea's smile had given him.

She didn't just have brown hair, she had long flowing hair that
made a man want to touch it. Wrap it around his fingers.

Drea's eyes weren't just brown, they were open and playful
and naughty. What kind of man could resist that full-on sexy
combination?

And while she might be average in height, when she wrapped
her arms around his neck and fitted that surf-toned body of hers
to his, he was a goner.

He should end this right now. What was going on between
them wasn't professional. It wouldn't be good for him or for her.
But how fair was that? Drea clearly needed that sponsorship, and
how could he deny her the opportunity just because he didn't
want to keep his hands off her?

She deserved a sponsorship. She was a good surfer, and it was
no fluke she'd earned her Rookie of the Year status. She had guts
and amazing instinct. What she lacked was the style and caution
to earn the points from the judges while keeping herself safe. He
wanted to help her, he truly did, and not just because he found

her sexy, or because she kissed him in such a way that he forgot about business or surfing or discipline for the first time since he could remember. He wanted to help her because he liked her and saw a little something of himself, that drive that made her want to push and push herself until she reached the top.

He admired her and desired her all at the same time, and that was a problem.

When he'd set himself down this path, his goal was to help new surfers in and out of the water. Could he give her the sponsorship and walk away from training her himself?

IT WAS three o'clock and the tourists were milling about the Trading Post oohing over the dancing hula-girl dolls, trying on the brightly colored Hawaiian shirts and picking out postcards. Drea was slipping a credit card receipt into the bin below the cash register she'd finally mastered when a large bound stack of papers landed on the counter.

Startled, she looked up to see Kirk's smiling face.

"What is that?" she asked, excitement racing through her body.

"A contract."

"Really?" she asked so loudly several of the customers jerked their heads her way.

He leaned over the counter, getting eye to eye with her. "I would have offered you the sponsorship this morning, but I needed to do some thinking."

"About my surfing?"

His gaze lowered to her mouth. "About that kiss."

"Oh," she said, feeling warm all over despite the heavy blast of air-conditioning.

Something fierce burned deep in his green eyes. "That kiss changed everything. Suddenly, offering you that sponsorship didn't seem professional anymore. Still, you need protection, and that contract will give you that."

"Protection? Why?"

"You need to know that the Da Kine sponsorship doesn't ride on you playing in the water with the boss."

"I never thought that." She rushed to reassure him, but she'd never be able to make herself feel sorry for kissing him.

His shoulders relaxed and his smile seemed a little more easy. Had he been worried she'd only kissed him, flirted with him because she wanted his money? She'd be insulted if that weren't probably his reality. Her mother had always said being rich rather than poor only traded one set of problems for another.

Although she wouldn't mind trying out the rich-person problems for a while.

"What you're signing is an agreement between Da Kine and you. Not me. Anytime you want to leave, you can, provided you do it in writing. If the lawyers representing Da Kine want to end the sponsorship, the conditions are clearly outlined, as is the protocol. I can't fire you, Drea. The sponsorship is yours, if you want it. It's not contingent on…"

"Kissing the boss?" she asked with a laugh.

"No."

Silly as it sounded, a lump formed in her throat. Kirk had gone to this extra trouble to protect her, to make sure everything was aboveboard. He didn't have to do it. He could have given his sponsorship to someone who offered fewer…complications. If he had, she would have still wanted to see him privately. Surely she was that obvious.

Those extra provisions were the nicest things anyone had ever done for her. Drea saw a whole new side of him. Kirk Murray was a man of honor, and that would have sounded corny, but right now she'd never wanted to be with someone more. That crush was turning into something more. Way more.

Keep it light. Keep it simple.

She tapped the contract with her nail. "So, technically, once I sign this, I could kiss you whenever I wanted."

"Technically. Sure," he said with a shrug. "No one's stopping you."

"Powell, what's going on?"

Drea straightened and addressed the booming voice calling

her name. "Kirk Murray, this is Larry Cronin, my boss here at the Trading Post."

Larry raised one of his shaggy brows. "Surfer?"

Kirk nodded.

"Just a few more minutes, okay?" she asked.

Her boss pursed his lips, then adjusted a display of Hawaiian coffee. "Five minutes," he agreed, then walked off.

"Interesting guy," Kirk told her.

"Not used to being so easily dismissed, are you?" she asked as she grabbed a rag to wipe the counter, hoping it would make her look busy.

"You think this is funny." His tone almost sounded accusatory.

"It must be hard to not be treated as if you're Kirk Murray, champion surfer. Or Kirk Murray, son of one of the richest men on the island."

"How about Kirk Murray, boyfriend?"

She stopped wiping and met his green eyes. "Hmmm, that has a ring to it," she said, opting for casual. But her heart beat faster.

He pushed the contract toward her. "I tried to make this as fair as possible, but still you should have your lawyer look at it."

Yeah, I'll have my whole team right on it.

She nodded as she took the papers from him. Her fingers shook. This contract represented everything she'd wanted. Worked for.

"Enough with the chitchat, Powell. Back to work," Larry called from across the store.

"Am I going to get you into trouble?" Kirk asked.

"Don't worry about it. I have a feeling I won't be working here much longer." She couldn't stop smiling or keep the excitement out of her voice.

"According to the agreement, you'll receive your first paycheck a week from Friday, but maybe we can get you a bridge loan. You'll need to get publicity shots and suit fittings before the competition," Kirk explained.

"New suits?" No more clearance rack. No more stretched-out, salt-damaged and sun-bleached bikinis.

"Featuring the Da Kine logo."

"Of course," she said, grinning.

"We can talk about that tonight. I'll pick you up at eight. My parents are having a cocktail party at the hotel lounge."

"Powell."

"He's leaving," she called good-naturedly, but right now she felt as if she were floating on a cloud. That's how good she felt.

"See you tonight, Drea."

Kirk left her with two thoughts. First, she hadn't said yes to going out with him tonight. And second…what the hell would *she* wear to a cocktail party?

4

BETWEEN Kaydee, Laci and JC, Drea was outfitted in a simple black backless dress. "These strappy heels are the perfect touch. Thanks for all your help, Kaydee," Drea said as she turned away from the full-length mirror to smile at her friends.

"The one who's going to need help is Kirk Murray. You look stunning," JC said with a laugh.

"I can't believe I agreed to go to a cocktail party," Drea said, adjusting the skirt.

"You'll do great."

Right on cue, there was a knock at the door. Drea rushed to answer it and her mouth nearly dropped open. She'd seen Kirk in swim trunks on the beach, casual at his restaurant and now in a dark suit and tie and carrying a yellow hibiscus. Talk about stunning.

After a quick round of introductions, Kirk escorted her to his car, the kind of vehicle that was probably worth more than she'd ever earned. Soft leather seats, navigation system and the kind of stereo that would have made her high-school boyfriend cry.

"Don't take this the wrong way, but your place looked kind of small. Where do you sleep?" he asked once they were on the road.

"Oh, Kaydee doesn't live there. She's a business student at the Western Oahu campus. She's been using me as her marketing project." Was he asking about the sleeping arrangements out of curiosity or for more personal reasons? Her mouth went a little dry thinking about those very personal reasons.

"Two roommates, a job and now this friend you're helping. That's a lot of distractions. How can you train that way?"

"Believe me, I've had to do a lot worse to keep my head above water," she said, chuckling.

Kirk didn't join in. "I'm not sure that you should. You're about to enter a major competition. You need restorative sleep. Time to focus."

"Is that like merging with a wave?"

"Drea, I'm serious. Things are different now. It's not just about you. You represent Da Kine. You have to be in peak physical condition. Not to mention looking good for your publicity shots. Not that you'll have any trouble looking fantastic, but bags under your eyes will not translate well onto a poster."

"I understand, but there's nothing much I can do about it." Hawaii was notorious for its high prices and sharing a place to stay came with the bargain of living on the circuit.

With a press of some buttons on the steering wheel, a phone, set on Speaker, was ringing. "Makana Hotel."

"Hi, James, it's Kirk Murray. I need a suite for the next two weeks."

"Certainly, Mr. Murray. We're booked tonight, but with a little finesse I'll have an opening tomorrow. Beachfront?"

"Finesse away. Put it under the name of Andrea Powell."

"Ahh, the daredevil rookie. Your father mentioned you might be looking for new ventures. I take it things are working out."

He smiled before he answered, and Drea felt like grinding her teeth.

"Really well."

With another push of the buttons, the call ended. Although she knew it was a mistake, Drea didn't wait to count to ten before turning on him. "I can't believe you just did that."

"Did what? James has been working in our hotel for years. It's no big deal."

"You could have asked. Maybe talked with me about it." She took a deep breath and glanced out her window. Watched palm trees whizz by.

"The Makana is right off the beach. No surfers' changes in the car. Showers in your own place. I thought you'd be happy."

"I understand what you were trying to do, but you can't take over. *That* wasn't what I expected when I signed the contract."

With a flick of his wrist, he signaled and turned into the parking lot of a large high-rise hotel. The Makana. Her new home for the next two weeks, starting tomorrow. He pulled his car out of the way of traffic, put it in Park and faced her.

"This sponsorship thing is new to me. I saw a problem and I wanted to fix it. But Drea, you can't tell me you wanted to keep sharing with your friends. This way you'll have the quiet you need to focus, and room service."

Her eyes widened. "No more cooking? I can't remember the last time I ate something I didn't have to cook. Not that soup or macaroni and cheese is all that hard."

"Then what's the problem?"

"Laci and JC, they're part of the competition surf crowd. All those girls know each other. They're friends. I'm just…just an interloper. Which is fine, I'm used to it, believe me. I was always the new girl in school. The new employee, the new whatever. Staying with Laci and JC sort of eased my transition."

Understanding entered his eyes, and his expression softened. "The surf crowd is your crowd now. You need to start building those networks without using Laci and JC as a crutch. They won't always be there."

Kirk was right. She knew it. Drea just didn't want to start working on those friendships. She was much more comfortable with the loner role she'd cast herself in.

He reached for her hand and gave it a squeeze. "How about if I promise to not make decisions like that again, if you promise to give this living arrangement a try. If you don't like it, we'll leave."

"And you won't be weird about it?"

"I'll buy you the can of chicken noodle myself."

She squeezed his hand back. "Thanks."

"Glad we got that out of the way. Our first fight."

They both laughed. Their relationship, or whatever it could be called, was certainly on the fast track.

"Now we can get to the best part of a fight," he teased.

"The making-up part?"

He leaned over, his lips just inches from hers. "A woman who gets my meaning." Then his mouth lightly brushed against hers. She felt the warmth of his breath on her cheek. Inhaled the exotic scent of his cologne. Her mouth watered whenever she caught the scent of one of Hawaii's native plants, but the scent on Kirk made her want to close her eyes and breathe in deeply.

"I've wanted to kiss you ever since you opened the door and I saw you standing there in this dress looking gorgeous. Hell, I wanted to kiss you at the Trading Post."

"Then why are you talking?" she asked against his lips.

He didn't waste time answering her question. Instead, his fingers curved around her shoulders and his lips took hers. This wasn't the soft, exploring kiss on the beach. This was a kiss of want and desire and passion, but most especially promise. A promise of more to come. She liked the thought of it. Liked it a lot.

But slowly he pulled away. "As awkward as dragging you into the backseat would be, I'd be willing to do it if I didn't know my parents were waiting for us inside, or that there are security cameras installed throughout the parking lot."

Drea's groan turned into a giggle.

Kirk turned away and gripped the steering wheel. Had she done that to him? Made him need to wait and get himself under control? She liked that, because he'd made her breath catch, and her heart beat to the kind of level even surfing didn't match.

With a smile, she adjusted the straps of her dress. Then she pulled down the mirror to make sure her lipstick wasn't smeared.

He started the car, and pulled into the valet parking area. After handing the keys to the valet, he escorted Drea through the lobby and to a lounge.

"Spend a lot of time here?" she asked.

"I practically grew up here." He opened the door and Drea almost lost her balance. She'd never seen such a beautiful room. One whole side was lined with doors opening up to the incredible beach view, lit by flaming tiki torches. Gorgeous chandeliers hung from the ceiling and dark Pacific wood accented the elegant surroundings.

In a word, the view, the room, the hotel was luxurious. And the people inside the room all matched. The women wore elegant updos, while the men sported suits that would pay for a new board.

And more.

Kirk must have sensed her natural inclination to flee because the reassuring warmth of his hand suddenly rested on the small of her back. "Come on, I'll introduce you to my parents."

If she thought the physical setting was intimidating, then actually seeing Kirk's family up close was downright scary. His mom had that picture-perfect elegance that appeared as natural to her as breathing, and his father wore an air of wealth.

For a moment, she wondered if she wore an air of poverty.

A waiter walked by with a tray of something that looked alcoholic, and Drea was really tempted.

His parents were all polite smiles and welcome, but then his father took Kirk aside to talk business. Drea wandered around to further check out the room. A large buffet was tucked in the corner. All kinds of fruit were on display, but she wasn't hungry.

She'd lost her appetite because she was facing the fact that she didn't belong here. She probably didn't belong with Kirk. The man was out of her league—

No. She wouldn't go there. Her mother hadn't raised her to think that way about herself. These people were rich and had probably known which fork and spoon to use since they could hold a utensil, but they weren't better than she was.

They just had nothing in common with her.

Just like Kirk. The only thing that brought them into the same sphere was surfing.

And desire.

Whenever she wanted something, she went after it full force, with everything she had, no matter what anyone said. She wanted Kirk Murray, and she wasn't going to let money, or her lack of it, or her strange reaction to it make her back away from him now.

She scanned the room for Kirk and spotted him by an ice sculpture. He seemed miserable as he tugged at his tie, talking to two men. She wanted to take that tie off. Pull the knot apart and slowly slide the material out of the collar. She could almost hear the whisper as the fabric moved, feel the heat from the friction.

Just then Kirk glanced up. His eyes met hers, then narrowed. He must have seen the white-hot desire in her gaze. Her need. Her determination. With a quick word, he stalked toward her, leaving the man he was with in midconversation.

"Ready to go?" he asked when he reached her side.

"We've only been here fifteen minutes," she said, her tone innocent.

"I don't care," he replied, his voice rough and strained.

Excitement and desire flooded through her. Made her nipples tighten. Her panties felt restrictive. "Then let's get out of here."

"Back to the bungalow?" he asked, his face tight with tension.

"Your place?"

"Excellent idea." She felt the familiar weight of his hand at the small of her back as he gently but quickly guided her out of the room.

"Don't you want to say goodbye to your parents?"

"No."

Their rush through the hotel, into the car and to his place happened in a blur. All she knew was the second he shut the door behind him with his foot, she was putting into action her fantasy of taking off his tie.

With a push to his broad shoulders, she had him up against the living-room wall, her fingers at his tie. She tugged at the knot, not very well since she didn't have a lot of experience with men who wore the things. But finally, *finally* she had one end free, reveling in the sound of the silk sliding against the cotton of his collar, just as she imagined. She couldn't wait to get at the first button.

His warm hands slid up her legs, pushing her black skirt higher and higher. She shivered when his fingers reached her thighs, making it hard to focus on the buttons of his shirt. He hooked her leg up around his waist, and she moaned as she felt the hardness of his erection against her most sensitive place.

"Do that again," he urged, his voice husky and seductive.

"Do what?" she asked.

"Make that sound."

"Make me make it," she challenged.

Surprise darkened his eyes, then determination. Kirk seemed to be the kind of a man who always got his way, and she was just the kind of woman who'd make him work for what he wanted.

His fingers slid from her thighs to cup her ass. The heat from his hands seared her through the barely there black panties she wore. His eyes never left hers as he pulled her closer, rubbing her once more.

She moaned, and her eyes drifted shut. Drea didn't even care that he'd gotten his way. How he made her feel was just too good. Actually, she *had* made him work for it, she realized with a smile.

"What's that smile for?" he asked.

She slowly raised her gaze to meet the intensity in his eyes. "You."

He opened his mouth as if he wanted to say something, then he groaned. He cupped her face, drawing her lips toward his own.

Wild and hungry, they kissed and kissed until only the harsh sound of their breathing filled the air. She forgot everything about tonight but the calloused heat of his hands on her skin and the delicious taste of his mouth.

He broke his lips from hers. With frustration and disappointment, she tried to reach for him, bring his mouth back to hers. Until she felt his lips lower to the line of her jaw.

Below her ear.

To the soft responsive side of her neck.

"I can feel how hard your heart is beating."

He gently licked the sensitive pulse point, and her knees went a little weak. Actually went weak. She'd chide herself later, but she'd probably do it again if given the chance. And again.

He moved his hands to her hips to keep her balanced. "Check out this aerial," he said, and spun her until she faced the wall.

She'd been impressed by his aerials on his surfboard, but this move was far more thrilling. And electrifying to her senses.

Kirk placed her hands above her head. "Keep them there," he ordered.

There he went again, telling her what to do. She'd let him get away with it this time. Only because she wanted to know where this would lead.

He traced a slow path down her arms that she felt all the way to her fingertips. When he reached her breasts he lightly touched them. The wings of a butterfly would have been more forceful. She swallowed her growing need for a more powerful touch, knowing that when he finally delivered, the wait would make it all the sweeter. Then he cupped her breasts. She moaned at his touch.

"That's what I've been waiting to hear."

"Next time don't take so long," she said.

He chuckled, the warmth of his breath on the back of her neck sending a shiver down between her shoulders.

He softly caressed her breasts, played with her nipples through her clothes.

"You are the sexiest thing I've ever seen. I've thought of nothing but touching you," he said. The hard ridge of his erection grew and she arched her back to feel it more. The sound of his groan sent a wave of hot sensation all through her body, so she arched again. She loved knowing she could drive him wild.

"Then touch me. Touch me everywhere," she urged, her voice sounding achy.

A cool rush of air hit her bare legs, and she realized one of his hands had left her breast to raise her skirt. Her thighs tingled with the soft graze of his fingers. Then she felt his slow touch at the edge of her panties.

Get there, already.

Kirk laughed deep in his throat as if he understood her frustration. Wanted to prolong it. So she arched her back again, and his fingers drifted under the elastic.

He cupped her, and her knees went weak once more. His fingers lightly stroked her clit. "Yes. There," she urged.

But he slipped his hand away, and guided her to the large couch, which dominated the living room. They fell across the soft leather of the armrest. Draped over the edge of the furniture like this meant that even if her legs failed her, she wouldn't fall to the carpeted floor. His foot gently pushed her feet apart so he could have better access to her body. His hand slid into her panties once again and she moaned. She balanced on the tips of her toes and his erection once again pressed against her backside.

He stroked her clit with a light, tantalizing touch, then his fingers moved lower. Into her. She tried to bite back the moan, but why fight it? The sensations he aroused in her were not supposed to be quiet.

Kirk developed a rhythm with his fingers. Around her clit, then in and out. Over and over again. She gripped the cushion under her hands as he whispered into her ear. "That's it, Drea. Grind against me, and I'll make you feel so good."

She pushed against him hard, and he slid a finger into her while his thumb took over caressing the best spot.

"Come," he said. His voice, his hands, his warmth an invitation.

Her muscles tensed and she squeezed her eyes tight.

She gasped as she orgasmed, her whole body trembling from the force of her body's release.

Kirk licked behind her ear. "I could listen to you make that sound all day long. Let me do it again."

"No," she said as she grabbed his arm. With her wavering strength, she pulled his hand from her panties, turned and backed along the couch until she was lying fully against the soft gray cushions. "Make love to me, Kirk."

She watched as he shrugged out of his dress shirt, then the T-shirt he'd worn underneath. It probably sounded corny as hell, but he was a thing of beauty—made the way a man was supposed to be made. She'd seen his naked chest a lot, touched it even. But somehow, knowing he was about to be joined to her in the most intimate way two people could be joined, she appreciated his body on a whole new level.

"Sure you don't want the bed?"

Drea shook her head. "No. Right here." She pulled the dress up and over her head, tossing it to the carved coffee table to emphasize her point.

She watched Kirk swallow, then reach for his wallet to take

out a condom. His pants and underwear joined his shirt on the floor and she watched as he rolled the latex down his hard length. That simple act alone would make her ready for his penetration. She reached up, wanting to finish the job for him. Wanting to feel the hardness of his cock in her hand.

His gaze met hers when her fingers joined his, then his eyes closed and he groaned when she slid the condom firmly in place.

"You're still wearing too many clothes."

With a smile, Drea hooked her fingers on the elastic at her hips, then slowly slid the black silk down her legs. The skin around his mouth tightened with each inch.

"You're going to pay for that," he said, his tone holding tempting promise.

She crooked her finger at him in invitation.

He lowered himself onto her, then pressed inside. Nothing felt like the weight of a man. *Nothing.* She welcomed him, wrapping her legs around his back once he was fully inside. He felt incredible. Hard and hot and just what she wanted. Needed.

He cupped her face once more and kissed her. His tongue mimicked the movements of his body as he slowly thrust into her.

But Drea didn't want slow. She pushed at his shoulders and he sat up, taking her with him. Seated atop him, she could now control the angle, the speed. His lips found her nipple, and she lowered herself onto his erection, wanting to give him a taste of his own slow performance. He gently grazed her breast with his teeth, and suddenly she didn't care about teasing him. Drea began to move.

It didn't take her long to reach her peak, and her movements became more frenzied. He cupped her backside, guiding her and bringing her down on him with force. Her inner muscles began to grip him as her orgasm took over. She held him tighter, wanting him closer. Sensation exploded inside her. Stronger, more powerful than the previous climax. She gasped for air, feeling him get harder and harder inside her. Then his whole body tensed, and he came with a deep, satisfied groan.

Drea's head lowered to his shoulder. They were both sweaty,

their bodies sensitive from the rush of orgasm. After a while, he gently pulled away from her body and lowered them both to the couch. She settled against the tight muscles of his chest as he buried his face in her hair. She basked in the feel of his solid body alongside hers. How long they lay there she didn't know, but he kissed her lips and her eyes fluttered open.

"Good?" he asked.

"Very good," she told him with a slow smile.

"The couch," he said, disgust filling his voice. "I can't believe we didn't make it to the bedroom."

"Are you knocking it?"

"Never. One of my best new memories just happens to have been made on a couch."

5

IF KIRK were the epitome of the fierce and tender lover the night before, under the morning sun with a surfboard under him, he'd become a tyrant. Talk about morning-after regrets.

"Make your pop-up more fluid."

"Your hands are too close to the board."

"Make your footwork more precise when you do your cross-over."

And they still had the videos to analyze.

On and on it went, and to top it off, she now had some jerk paddling behind her, ready to steal her position and horn in on her wave. Surfers called these jerks snakes, and she thought that name really fit.

She managed to take care of business and ride the wave. Kirk motioned her toward the shore, and she grabbed her board and met him at the sand. She dreaded what she'd hear, hating the change in their relationship. It was as if he'd taken all that control and focus he was so fond of and directed it solely at her flaws.

His expression was harsh. "What were you doing out there? You were far too aggressive with the other surfers."

"Are you talking about that snake? You're the one who talks about being one with the water and respect for the ocean. If the water's crowded, I'm happy to wait my turn, but I'm not giving any handouts."

A series of emotions played across his face. Then she visibly saw the tension release from his shoulders. "You're right," Kirk said after a moment.

"What?" she asked, raising her eyebrows and deliberately

giving her tone a touch of incredulousness. "Did you just say I'm right? After everything being wrong from my stance to how I angle, I'm doing something that works for you?"

A small smile played about the ruggedness of his mouth. "Is that how I sounded?"

That slight tug of his lips made up for a lot of his tyrannical attitude. "A little."

"A lot." His eyes narrowed. "Listen, Drea. You have amazing surf instincts. You're a winner, but you are missing the refinements, the little things that give you those extra style points from the judges. But I don't want to change you. How you handled that surfer reminded me that your style is aggressive. You don't have to do everything I say, or adopt my attitude, but I do want you to give it a try. To take it under consideration."

She met his green gaze, and nodded. "I will."

"Especially since I'm right."

She swung her head in his direction, studied his expression. Then Drea gasped. "Did you just make a joke? Kirk Murray just made a joke about the seriousness that is surfing. I can't believe it."

"I make jokes all the time."

"Are you sure? Because I think sometimes you forget that surfing is supposed to be fun."

He instantly returned to the serious trainer. "It's a sport. A very dangerous sport if you don't take it seriously. Don't forget the motto. Respect the wave—"

"Respect the sport. I remember."

He'd quoted it often enough today.

She took a deep breath, missing their special connection of the day before. And especially of the night. "I know it's Da Kine, but it's you, too. I know I can never repay you for what you've done for me. You're going to teach me style, I'm going to teach you to have a little fun in your life."

"Now that, wahine, is something I'm going to take you up on." His voice sent shivers down her back. Here she was thinking about the fun of standing on a board, and now he had her thinking of fun between the sheets. He'd never called her wahine before. The endearment men used for female surfers.

She leaned against him. "I like it when you speak Hawaiian to me." She liked it a lot.

His gaze darkened, but then his expression turned regretful, and he glanced down at his watch. "Ready to say goodbye to your new roommates?"

No.

Instead she smiled and nodded.

Kirk had met her at the beach, grumbling about dawn patrol. She hadn't wanted to make a lot of noise moving out this morning, so they were waiting until after they'd completed their surfing to remove her things from the bungalow.

"You do have to admit the beach is less crowded now," she told him.

His hand slid around her hip. "I'd trade the crowds for more time in bed. With you."

Drea had spent most of the night at Kirk's, knowing her roommates, and probably Kaydee for that matter, would be wanting a full report about her date. Lucky for her, they'd been asleep when she'd finally slipped inside the bungalow. Her feelings were too new to want to talk about them.

"It's crazy you doing dawn patrol anyway."

"I told you, I can't quit the Trading Post. I promised Mr. Cronin two weeks notice, and I need to keep good relations with him in case…"

Kirk's lips tightened. "Okay, now we're getting to the real reason. You were going to say you needed to keep good relations in case your surfing doesn't take off?"

Or the sponsorship dissolves? But she'd keep that thought to herself.

"Drea, why are you afraid to think things might just work out?"

Why did everyone want to analyze her motivations?

"You have to keep a positive frame of mind at all times."

"That's easy for you to say. You've always had Daddy's money…" She let her words trail off.

"I always had Daddy's money to fall back on. That's what you were going to say."

She gave him a quick nod.

Kirk gave an easy shrug. "It's true. I've had it easier than most. That's the reason why I want to sponsor and train surfers. Give them the same kind of shot I had."

"Like what you're doing with me."

"Like what I'm *trying* to do with you. You have to start believing in yourself to make it work."

She flashed him a big smile. "I promise to try harder."

She could tell he didn't believe her for a second, but he did visibly relax. "Come on, let's get your stuff from the bungalow."

There was believing in herself and there was also being realistic. Keeping her job at the Trading Post was being realistic. Remembering that Kirk Murray wouldn't always be her financial savior was also being realistic.

Even though she'd almost put her foot in her mouth, she was glad they'd had this conversation. She'd realized something about Kirk today. Although he took her comment about his daddy's money in stride, she knew she'd struck a small nerve. Maybe that's why he was so focused and almost businesslike about his surfing. Money might have put him in the position to get his shot, but Kirk's winning was all him.

Strange that they had something in common. She wanted to prove that Rookie of the Year wasn't a fluke. He wanted to prove he was the real deal. He'd met his goal. She'd just have to think positively about hers. Kirk would be proud.

LACI AND JC were waiting for her in the living room of the bungalow. She'd met both of them briefly in California, where she'd won her title, but she hadn't hung around after the awards ceremony to chat. She just never seemed to fit in with the other surfers. But the pair had been a lifesaver when she'd arrived in Hawaii with little more than her board and no place to stay. They'd offered her their third bedroom. She'd thought they viewed her as little more than a pest, but now that she was actually moving out, the two looked a little down. Were they upset about her leaving?

JC stood and picked up one of Drea's bags, handing it to her. "Thanks," Drea said.

"No problem."

They were about the same height, but that's where the similarities ended. JC, who had had a meteoric rise to the top, enjoyed the gorgeous, exotic looks that made her a favorite among the male surfers and potential sponsors.

"Anything I can help with?" Laci asked as she passed Drea's other bag to Kirk. She had that summery all-American girl look, with a face full of freckles.

"That's it? Just two bags?" Kirk asked.

"I'm an efficient packer," Drea said in a poor attempt at humor.

Laci turned toward Kirk. "Drea doesn't have any clothes."

"I have clothes." But that defensive statement sounded pretty weak even to her own ears.

JC flashed her a secret wink. "Not the right kind of clothes. You'll be doing interviews, community-service time. Shorts and T-shirts don't work."

"And don't forget the evening stuff," Laci added.

"I can't believe I hadn't thought of that. I've already ordered new suits and rashguards with the Da Kine logo," Kirk said.

"She's going to need the works," JC told him.

"I'm on it." Kirk grabbed his phone.

"Do I really need that stuff?" Drea just wanted to surf. Surely Kirk wouldn't want her before cameras and reporters so soon. She hadn't taken any of the publicity training Kaydee had insisted she'd need, and Drea wasn't exactly a natural with a microphone in front of her face. Memories of how she'd frozen up in front of a high-school classmate flashed through her mind. The reporter was a friend just trying to get her yearbook class assignment completed. Imagine how terrible she'd do if it were for real. She'd let down Da Kine and Kirk.

"Trust me, you're going to want all those clothes. The reporters will be all over you," Laci said with a nod.

With a click, Kirk returned his cell phone to the latch on his belt. "Okay, you're all set for four at the store in my father's hotel. I hate to rush things, but I have to get to work."

Drea nodded, but made no move. The room grew quiet. The four of them just looked at one another awkwardly.

Beside her, Kirk stood straighter, as if he'd just realized something. "I'll put these in the trunk so you all can talk. Just come out when you're ready, Drea."

"Please tell me you have hooked up with that man, because to not do so would be a sad and terrible waste," Laci said when Kirk was out of earshot.

Drea felt the heat in her cheeks and knew she was blushing. "I, uh…"

"Don't bother answering. Your face tells us nothing is going to waste. What I can't believe is that you came back here last night when you could have spent all night in bed with him," JC said. Then she glanced toward Laci. "A whole new wardrobe. Pretty slick."

"What can I say?" Laci said, grinning.

Drea leaned against the wall. "I can't believe it myself. It's like from a movie, and at four o'clock, that's where the fun, pumpy music comes in, and the girl comes out of the dressing room, flashing from one exciting outfit to the next while her friends shake their heads or smile."

"I can shake my head," JC said.

Laci nodded. "I can smile."

Looked as if she was going to have help shopping. Good. She hadn't figured it out until just this moment that she had stopped thinking of JC and Laci as competitors and roommates and now thought of them as true friends.

"I'm going to miss you guys," she said quietly, feeling her throat tighten.

JC gave her a quick hug. "Hey, it's not like we're not going to see you every day on the beach."

"And feel free to invite us over for room service anytime," Laci told her with a smile. "We were counting on your skills with the can opener."

Drea gave them both a hug, then quickly walked out to the car where Kirk was waiting for her.

As she shut the car door, Kirk reached for her hand and gave her a squeeze. "Okay?"

She nodded, but quickly changed the subject. "We surfing tomorrow?"

"Actually, I thought we could review the tape of today's surfing."

She raised a brow. "And where would we be doing that? Some place like, oh, your apartment?"

Kirk nodded. "My apartment works."

Drea laughed. "I'm looking forward to it."

The laughter faded from his eyes, replaced by heat and sexual tension. His fingers brushed her cheek. "If I kiss you now, I may just drag you to my apartment."

Drea leaned across the gearshift and puckered.

Kirk groaned. "Wahine, you are going to kill me. I have to go to work."

Warmth from his words suffused her body. "Drive," she said, smiling. "I can kill you tomorrow."

KIRK WASN'T SURPRISED when his dad walked into the small room Kirk used as an office at the back of Da Kine.

"You cut out of there pretty early last night. Your mother barely had the chance to say two words to you."

"Good one, Dad. Zeroed right in on the surefire guilt inducer," Kirk said as he saved the spreadsheet he was preparing and spun in his chair to face his dad.

John Murray nodded as if he was taking a small bow. "You really do need to spend more time at the hotel. Someday it will all be yours."

"You have plenty of years to run your hotel, I'm not worried about taking up the reins. Besides, I had to get Drea home. She's training."

"Very stunning young woman. You're sponsoring surfers now?" But it wasn't really a question. His father knew exactly what his child was doing. "When you'd first mentioned looking toward ventures outside of surfing, it was only to help train other surfers. You have the restaurant, you're sponsoring and now it looks like you're still in training. What about your retirement?"

"It's buildup to the retirement. Da Kine is doing the sponsoring, and it's all part of the business plan. I've made an agreement with XtremeSportNet and the Girls Go Banzai competition. The restaurant is now the official meal provider for all the competitors, staff and other corporate sponsors."

The other man nodded. His father's unique version of "well done." "Impressive, and good experience for when you take over the hotel. But how does Da Kine sponsoring a surfer figure into the deal?"

Kirk imagined Drea in her new suit, and his body instantly became more aware. Edgy. "She'll be wearing the logo, and believe me when I tell you it will be seen a lot. Drea Powell is going to be a star. Have you seen her surf? She's amazing. Gutsy. We're training together."

Although he couldn't help noticing the panic that entered her eyes when interviews came into conversation. He'd wanted to tell her she'd be great, not just with an audience. The two of them hadn't even discussed how they wanted to proceed together in public. He would have been thrilled with showing the world she was the woman by his side, but he wouldn't without talking it over with her first. He smiled as he remembered her anger at him making the decision about where she was going to live. He wouldn't fall into that trap again.

"Surfing was always your area of expertise, so I'll take your word on it." John Murray's eyes grew concerned. "Things looked a little more…*personal* between the two of you than just a business arrangement."

Had he been that obvious last night?

Hmmm, what had given him away? The fact that he couldn't stop touching her or that they'd stayed fifteen minutes before he ushered her out of the lounge as fast as he could? The sex that had followed lived up to way more than his expectations. "Dad, I—"

"No need to explain. I was your age once. There was a time with your mother—"

Kirk held up a hand, grimacing. "Dad, these are really not details I want to know."

His dad smiled. "Probably not. As my son, I know how much you hate to take advice from your old man. But from one businessman to another, let me tell you—there's a reason for clichés like not mixing business with pleasure. It rarely works out."

"HEY THERE, surfer dude."

Kirk glanced up from the film he was watching to see Drea in his doorway.

Only it was a very different Drea. Dressed in a straight black skirt and silky, dark pink blouse, she didn't appear to be the wild and reckless surfer he knew.

The knot she'd twisted the soft, long strands of her hair into made him want to take out whatever pins she'd used to hold it in place and sink his face into the sweet-smelling strands.

The very appropriate length of her skirt made his fingers itch to find the clasp and feel the whoosh of air as the material drifted down her legs and hit the floor.

And those little tiny buttons on her shirt made him ache to undo each one and slide the material off her shoulders so he could admire her beautiful breasts.

Which was why it was a good thing he'd changed their meeting place from his apartment to his office at Da Kine.

The smile on her face was beginning to fade.

Oh, yeah. He'd been so caught up in thinking about how amazing she looked, he'd forgotten to say anything to her about it. "I could eat you up."

"Thank you," Drea said as she closed the door behind her and stalked to his desk. She wrapped her arms around his neck and leaned in for a kiss. "I've been thinking about doing this all day."

So had he. Working all day had been difficult, especially after hearing his father's words. He bent forward, his hands already reaching for the tempting buttons on her blouse. Until he remembered *he'd* sent her to get that blouse. And the rest of her professional attire.

"Wait, Drea, wait."

Her brows knitted in confusion. "What's wrong?"

"I think we may have rushed things." He hated saying that. Wished he could call the words back, but he'd been thinking about what his dad had said ever since he'd left. His father was a successful businessman, and his advice had always been spot-on.

He was expecting her to deny it, maybe even get defensive or reassure him. He hadn't expected her to laugh. "You think? Two days…" She made a tsking sound.

"I'm serious. You're in training now and need to concentrate. This is your first major competition since winning Rookie of the Year, and a relationship between us would be a huge distraction." Hard to say when all he wanted to do was, well, her.

She backed away and leaned against the wall. He hated seeing the pain in her eyes. Experiencing the same pain himself.

"That's why we have the contract. You think I can't handle it?" she asked, her voice filled with hurt.

"I've never actually trained anyone myself. I shouldn't allow myself to get distracted, either. We both need to be focused and controlled right now."

Drea folded her arms across her chest, and he thought she was going to argue with him. He almost wanted her to. Then she nodded and he reached for the remote control.

He hated that she didn't fight harder. That he hadn't, either.

Kirk powered up the TV. "Watch your stance on this first run you did."

The next six days followed the same pattern. Surfing in the morning, followed by dissecting the films of her runs at the restaurant in the afternoon. Gone was the sexy, irreverent woman of earlier. Drea had truly become more focused and her style was improving. Cutting off the sex had been the best decision for her career.

But it was the worst choice according to Kirk's body. If he'd thought seeing her splash around in the water in her bikini was tough a few days ago, now he knew what those small triangles of fabric hid.

His body physically ached as he positioned her hips on the board. He remembered how those hips felt against him as he thrust into her.

He missed her easy smiles, their conversation and her laughter. At night he stayed away, thinking of the soft, sexy sounds she made as she came.

Kirk was at a breaking point, which was ridiculous because two weeks ago he hadn't even known who Andrea Powell was, and now he couldn't concentrate on anything but her.

"Oh, look."

He glanced in the direction she pointed to see a young boy, his longboard twice as big as he was, struggling in the water. She smiled, and his breath caught and his gut clenched. That was the first smile he'd seen since he'd told her the personal side of their relationship had to end. He'd do just about anything to keep that smile on her face.

Drea asked, "Remember your first time on a board?"

He nodded. One of his nannies had brought him to the beach, so that she could meet up with her boyfriend, and Kirk had taken to surfing right away. Much to his father's horror. But that first time he rode a wave all the way to shore had been the best day of his life.

As a child. That memory couldn't compete with his evening with Drea.

"Let's help him," she suggested, and he quickly followed.

Kirk sensed that Drea was growing increasingly frustrated with her training. She was snapping. Her teasing responses were gone. As were the heated glances from her eyes and her quick smiles aimed at him. The break might do her good.

The boy's mom was trying to give him some pointers, but it was clear she didn't know how to guide him.

"Mind if we show him a few things?" Drea asked the woman.

"Hey, I know you," the woman said to Kirk. "You're that surf guy." A look of relief crossed the boy's mother's face. "Feel free. I'm terrible."

"Why don't you join us? You might have some fun." Then Drea turned to the boy. "My name's Drea and this is Kirk. What's your name?"

"I'm Riley."

"First thing, Riley, we're going to paddle on our board to grab that beach break. Have you ever ridden mush before?"

The boy laughed and shook his head.

"Well, you're going to."

An hour later the four of them were laughing and cheering as Riley popped up on his board and road the mushy white water of his first wave all the way in to shore. Riley hugged Drea and Kirk before they picked up their boards and made their way toward Kirk's car.

Drea handed her board to Kirk in silence, and he secured both boards to the racks on his car.

"That was a lot of fun," he said.

"Yeah, I've been missing fun."

She lifted her eyes to his, and his blood started to pound in his veins. Heat and desire were banked in those brown eyes of hers. And something else…something he could only describe as yearning.

"Have you?"

Without a thought, Kirk dragged her into his arms. His hands smoothed up and down her back. She fitted against him perfectly, so perfectly.

"I've thought of nothing else but this," she said.

Then he pushed her way. "Drea, we can't. You're supposed to be thinking of your training."

Drea glared at him. "Stop it, Kirk. Just stop it. Everything you've said to me since I moved into the hotel is about what I'm doing wrong. I can't live with my friends. I can't spend any time with you."

"What are you talking about? You're training with me."

"That's just it. Training. Your kind of training. I can't surf like this. I hate it. It's no wonder you're ready to quit. You've sucked every last bit of enjoyment and fun out of something that is supposed to be exhilarating and exciting."

Here it was, the crux of the problem between them. "And control and style. It's not about challenging the wave."

Drea made a scoffing sound. "You know what? I actually believe that part. Your whole one-with-nature, one-with-the-wave Zen thing I'm actually believing. But then I realized you don't *really* believe it. Not in your gut. Control isn't oneness, and it isn't me. I can't surf like this. And I won't."

"So what does this mean?" he asked, feeling panic. Was he losing her?

She pulled her hair from its clip, spreading it around her shoulders. Protecting herself. "I'm saying I'm releasing you from our contract. I'll put in writing as soon as possible. I think I'm just meant to go it alone."

She pivoted away, and he saw her wrap her arms around her waist. Kirk reached out for her, wanting to comfort her, but his hand fell to his side.

"I'm sorry," she went on, "I know I'm screwing up your sponsorship and publicity. I'll still wear my Da Kine surfwear if you want me to."

"Thanks," he said automatically, not knowing what to say or how to fix this. The woman he wanted, wanted to help, was walking away from him because she'd rather do that than keep working with him. It was like a kick to the stomach.

"If you'll take down my board, I'll head over to the bungalow."

"Walking?" He didn't like her walking so far. It wasn't safe.

She shrugged. "I've walked farther."

He just wanted to see her succeed. To hold her. And to be with her. He'd screwed up, and didn't understand how something so right had become messed up so badly. "I'll drive you."

Drea swallowed and she nodded. "Okay. Thanks."

Something in his tone must have suggested the supreme effort he was exerting not to argue with her any longer. She walked to the passenger side and slipped into his car.

He drove her to the bungalow for the last time. She didn't pause to give him a last look as she walked inside the house.

She was making a mistake, he thought. She was making the biggest mistake of her life. Yet two days later he realized he had it backwards. *He* was making the biggest mistake of his life.

6

HER HEAT was next.

Drea scanned the surf. The very still surf. Calm ocean. Beautiful to look at, fun for families with toddlers to frolic in...not good when you planned to surf on it. A light breeze, too light, brushed her face, and she kicked the warm sand at her feet.

Frustration with the situation made her muscles knot. This was her chance, her first time to surf with the big girls and prove that winning Rookie of the Year was not a fluke.

It was also her chance to prove that turning down Kirk's sponsorship had not been a huge blunder.

For the past forty-eight hours her thoughts were filled with the idea of knocking on Kirk's door and telling him that since she was no longer his trainee, they could go back to being lovers.

Pathetic.

She still wanted him, even though she'd tried not to.

Yeah, nothing was cooperating with her. Not the sea, not the man.

She sank to the sand and pulled out the surf schedule. The next big wave of competitions would take place in Australia, but there was no way she could even get there if she didn't win this competition. Everything was riding on Girls Go Banzai since no other offers of sponsorship had come her way, which was not surprising. What little she made at the Trading Post wouldn't be enough to get her to Sydney.

She had nothing left to sell, so she was stuck here in Hawaii. Not that being locked on one of the most beautiful places on earth was a hardship, but it was not exactly what she had in mind. Drea had to put some cash together.

Maybe she could give lessons. She'd enjoyed showing Riley how to surf, and it would keep her at the beach.

"It just keeps getting worse. We'll never get any good waves out of that," JC said as she joined Drea at her beach towel. "Here's your hot dog."

It was official, Drea Powell was back on the hot-dog budget. Good thing she hadn't really started to depend on room service.

JC was antsy and ready to hit the water. Girls Go Banzai had been good for her so far. She'd won the first heat outright, and Drea found herself genuinely happy for her. With her recent drop in the rankings, JC's confidence had been taking a beating.

"At least one good thing came out of this terrible weather, if low eighties and a light breeze could be considered terrible," Laci commented as she sank down on the sand beside her roommates. "Kirk's not here."

For the last two mornings, Kirk had surfed. He'd kept his distance, but twice Drea had thought she'd caught him looking in her direction. That wasn't surprising since every chance she'd gotten she'd been staring at him. A week ago, she would have risked it all and marched right up to him and asked why he was being such an idiot.

She was both angry and sad at the same time. A relationship could have worked between them while in training if *he'd* let it.

Yeah, a week ago she'd have confronted him. But not now. Something had changed. She just didn't want to figure it out. She stood, brushing the sand from her legs. "I think I'll go check with Linda and see if they've gotten any encouraging weather reports. Like a big tropical storm."

KIRK WAXED his surfboard as he waited for the weather to change. He'd always appreciated the familiar motions of prepping his board and stowing it away. But right now he was frustrated because he actually had the urge to rack it and head back to the beach. He truly wanted to hit the waves and surf.

Shock rocked him. He'd been feeling the drag of the professional surf circuit for a while, but he'd assumed he was just tired of the hotel rooms, the different cities and the travel. His dad convinced him he was ready to stay put in one place and do something different with his life.

And now he wasn't so sure that Drea didn't have a point. Maybe he was willing to give up his lifestyle because it wasn't fun for him anymore. Because he'd sucked the joy out of it.

Just as he'd done to Drea. His chest began to hurt.

His cell phone rang. It was Linda. "We've had some luck in the weather. The Pipeline is breaking eighteen feet, and your girl's up next."

Panic knifed through his gut. No way would Drea be able to resist eighteen feet, but it was crazy. The woman surfed like she had something to prove, and maybe he'd added to that need. He grabbed his car keys and headed to the competition.

When he arrived, large breaking waves were forming perfect barrels. Several surfers were already turning away from the lineup, intimidated by the height of the waves. Drea wasn't one of them.

THIS WAS IT. Her chance. The waves were crazy, and if Drea successfully surfed this monster, she'd win. Another sponsorship would surely be in her future then.

Daredevil.

Risk-taker.

Foolhardy.

The harsh words floated in her mind as she paddled out. The water hit her face and she arched to get a better view. More surfers were turning away. *Good.*

Control.

Focus.

She used to enjoy being alone with her own ideas on the water. Not anymore as Kirk's advice echoed in her thoughts and insisted on reminding her of his lessons.

Merge with the wave. Be one with it.

Now that was a suggestion of Kirk's she agreed with.

A huge swell headed her way. She closed her eyes and felt the vibration of the ocean through her board. Tried to be one with the wave.

She opened her eyes to see a bomb wave. And right now that wave was telling her to back off.

She had less than a second to decide.

Gripping tightly to her rails, Drea forced her weight to the side, inverting her board and submerging her head.

Her board took the brute force of the wave, propelling and dragging her toward shore.

She'd turned turtle. But that was better than being slammed and eating it.

Drea maneuvered her board and paddled back toward shore. She'd wiped out. Lost this chance to prove her skills as a surfer and an opportunity to impress enough to get a sponsorship in time to get to the next competition.

Laci met her at the shore with Drea's beach towel. "JC won."

Tired and a little beaten from the water, Drea was surprised that she felt real happiness for her new friend rather than just total disappointment for herself. This would be huge for JC.

"I'm glad you bailed, Drea. That wasn't safe."

Drea smiled because she liked hearing the relief and true concern in Laci's voice. "I think my daredevil days are over."

"Maybe you can keep just a bit. We wouldn't want you to completely change," Laci said with a wink. "I'm going to go congratulate JC. You coming?"

"I will in a minute." Right now Drea needed to be alone.

Nodding as if she understood her friend's unspoken thought, Laci waved and walked toward the competition's staging area.

Drea wrapped the towel tightly around her body like a cocoon and sank toward the sand.

"Hey, wahine."

Her body shivered. She missed his voice so much. *Great.* Kirk's appearance now just solidified her failure.

"I'm proud of you," he said quietly.

"I didn't win," she acknowledged, blinking back tears.

He lowered himself beside her, stretching out his long legs. "You did in a way. You proved something out there."

"How well I can turn turtle?"

"That you know when to back away from a wave, as well as when to take it on. That took guts and risk."

Cheering erupted and she knew they would be awarding JC her medal soon. A good friend would be there cheering, too.

"I wanted to win. I want it so bad, you don't know how much," she said, her voice thick with emotion. Her throat prickled with the effort to hold back the tears.

"Not winning is part of being a pro. In fact, you're going to lose far more often than you'll ever win. You need to come to terms with that now."

"I don't think I'll ever go pro. Not with my performance out there today."

Kirk reached for Drea's shoulders, the warmth of his fingers sinking into her skin. "That's where you're wrong. You're still Rookie of the Year, and as of ten minutes ago, you shed the one thing that was holding sponsors back. Your bad reputation."

Her back straightened. "I don't think my reputation was *that* bad."

His lips twisted into a smile. "Good. I much prefer outraged Drea over pity-party Drea."

She met his eyes. "Kirk, thank you for coming over here. I know it must have been awkward for you, and I want you to know I appreciate it. But you don't have to stay."

He leaned forward, his gaze boring into hers. "Are you trying to get rid of me?"

She'd already cried in front of the man, bared her emotions, she might as well go for the trifecta and share her feelings about him. "No, it's just hard for me with you being beside me."

There. She'd done it. Showed emotion. Given him an inkling that he could hurt her. That's why she'd never truly confronted him.

His gaze narrowed. "Why?" he asked, a strange urgency filling his voice.

"I mean, come on. What was I thinking? You don't fall in love with a person in a couple of days." *Okay, maybe not that truthful with my feelings.* She'd hide from analyzing that little gem, but she couldn't. She'd just blurted out that she'd fallen in love with him.

"Yeah, you do."

Drea's breath hitched and she glanced up. Kirk caught her face in his hands, tracing her lower lip with his thumb.

"I did," he said.

"You fell…" She couldn't finish the sentence. She wanted him to say it. To finish it.

"I fell in love with you."

Her heart pounded and she squeezed her eyes tight. Then she threw her arms around his neck. "Tell me again."

"I love you, Andrea Powell. It was the most uncontrolled, unfocused, risk-taking thing I've ever done, but there you go. Some of you is rubbing off on me."

She laughed.

"Why'd you stay away?"

He gazed out into the ocean. "At first I thought it was because you needed time. You were pretty mad and, let's face it, everything I said and did seemed to be wrong."

"Not everything," she remarked, reaching up for a kiss.

"Then I understand it was because I needed some time to adjust. I've lived my entire surf life with the same exact principles. They worked and I thought they'd work for you, too."

"Some of them did."

"And some of them did for me, too. But not all of them, and I was coming to understand that. That's why I've been so vague about my retirement. I wasn't really ready. I just wanted the fun back. I want *you* back."

"You have me."

And he lowered his mouth to kiss her. The kind of I-love-you, never-want-to-let-you-go kiss that made her ache for the two of them to be alone.

"What now? What do we do from here?" she couldn't help but ask.

He raised a brow. "What's this? Are you planning? Focusing?"

"Maybe some of you *is* rubbing off on me."

He took her hand, then stood, helping Drea to her feet. "Right now, we have someone to congratulate."

Drea scanned the podium. "I'm happy for her. She needed this win, just like I need you."

"And I need you."

"What about after the ceremony?" Drea reached for her board.

"Still more planning, I see. We have a surf circuit to do together."

"Together?" she asked, surprise lacing her voice. "So you're really not retiring. What about your restaurant?"

"Da Kine will be waiting when I return. When *we* return. The sponsorship is yours even if you kick me to the curb."

"That will never happen." Joy and excitement raced through her. She couldn't wait to start. Start her new life with Kirk *right now.* She strode toward the podium.

He grabbed her hands, his expression serious. With love shining from his eyes, he confessed, "You've given me something, Drea. Given me something back, actually. My love of surfing. I knew this morning that I'm looking forward to it again. I don't care if I win, if I lose, if my style is off. I'm just ready to surf again because I enjoy it, and you'll be right next to me."

"Being one with the wave."

Kirk draped his arm around her shoulders, and they began to walk down the beach together. "I knew you'd start seeing things my way."

"Yeah, just as much as you've started seeing mine."

He gave her hand a squeeze. "I'm going to look forward to this for the rest of my life."

* * * * *

*Celebrate 60 years of pure
reading pleasure with Harlequin!*

To commemorate the event, Harlequin Intrigue® is
thrilled to invite you to the wedding of The Colby Agency's
J. T. Baxley and his bride, Eve Mattson.

That is, of course, if J.T. can find the woman who left him
at the altar. Considering he's a private investigator for one
of the top agencies in the country—the best of the best—
that shouldn't be a problem. The real setback is that his
bride isn't who she appears to be...and her mysterious
past has put them both in danger.

*Enjoy an exclusive glimpse
of Debra Webb's latest addition to*
THE COLBY AGENCY:
ELITE RECONNAISSANCE DIVISION

THE BRIDE'S SECRETS

*Available August 2009
from Harlequin Intrigue®.*

The dark figures on the dock were still firing. The bullets cutting through the surface of the water without the warning boom of shots told Eve they were using silencers.

That was to her benefit. Silencers decreased the accuracy of every shot and lessened the range.

She grabbed for the rocks. Scrambled through the darkness. Bumped her knee on a boulder. Cursed.

Burrowing into the waist-deep grass, she kept low and crawled forward. Faster. Pushed harder. Needed as much distance as possible.

Shots pinged on the rocks.

J.T. scrambled alongside her.

He was breathing hard.

They had to stay close to the ground until they reached the next row of warehouses. Even though she was relatively certain they were out of range at this point, she wasn't taking any risks. And she wasn't slowing down.

J.T. had to keep up.

The splat of a bullet hitting the ground next to Eve had her rolling left. Maybe they weren't completely out of range.

She bumped J.T. He grunted.

His injured arm. Dammit. She could apologize later.

Half a dozen more yards.

Almost in the clear.

As she reached the cover of the alley between the first two warehouses she tensed.

Silence.

No pings or splats.

She glanced back at the dock. Deserted.

Time to run.

Her car was parked another block down.

Pushing to her feet, she sprinted forward. The wet bag dragged at her shoulder. She ignored it.

By the time she reached the lot where her car was parked, she had dug the keys from her pocket and hit the fob. Six seconds later she was behind the wheel. She hit the ignition as J.T. collapsed into the passenger seat. Tires squealed as she spun out of the slot.

"What the hell did you do to me?"

From the corner of her eye she watched him shake his head in an attempt to clear it.

He would be pissed when she told him about the tranquilizer.

She'd needed him cooperative until she formulated a plan. A drug-induced state of unconsciousness had been the fastest and most efficient method to ensure his continued solidarity.

"I can't really talk right now." Eve weaved into the right lane as the street widened to four lanes. What she needed was traffic. It was Saturday night—shouldn't be that difficult to find as soon as they were out of the old warehouse district.

A glance in the rearview mirror warned that their unwanted company had caught up.

Sensing her tension, J.T. turned to peer over his left shoulder.

"I hope you have a plan B."

She shot him a look. "There's always plan G." Then she pulled the Glock out of her waistband.

Cutting the steering wheel left, she slid between two vehicles. Another veer to the right and she'd put several cars between hers and the enemy.

She was betting they wouldn't pull out the firepower in the open like this, but a girl could never be too sure when it came to an unknown enemy.

Deep blending was the way to go.

Two traffic lights ahead the marquis of a movie theater provided exactly the opportunity she was looking for.

The digital numbers on the dash indicated it was just past midnight. Perfect timing. The late movie would be purging its audience into the crowd of teenagers who liked hanging out in the parking lot.

She took a hard right onto the property that sported a twelve-screen theater, numerous fast-food hot spots and a chain superstore. Speeding across the lot, she selected a lane of parking slots. Pulling in as close to the theater entrance as possible, she shut off the engine and reached for her door.

"Let's go."

Thankfully he didn't argue.

Rounding the hood of her car, she shoved the Glock into her bag, then wrapped her arm around J.T.'s and merged into the crowd.

With her free hand she finger-combed her long hair. It was soaked, as were her clothes. The kids she bumped into noticed, gave her death-ray glares.

They just didn't know.

As she and J.T. moved in closer to the building, she grabbed a baseball cap from an innocent bystander. The crowd made it easy. The kid who owned the cap had made it even easier by stuffing the cap bill-first into his waistband at the small of his back.

Pushing through the loitering crowd, she made her way to the side of the building next to the main entrance. She pushed J.T. against the wall and dropped her bag to the ground. Peeled off her T and let it fall.

His gaze instantly zeroed in on her breasts, where the cami she wore had glued to her skin like an extra layer. A zing of desire shot through her veins.

Not the time.

With a flick of her wrist she twisted her hair up and clamped the cap atop the blond mass.

"They're coming," J.T. muttered as he gazed at some point beyond her.

"Yeah, I know." She planted her palms against the wall on either side of him and leaned in. "Keep your eyes open. Let me know when they're inside."

Then she planted her lips on his.

* * * * *

Will J.T. and Eve be caught in the moment?
Or will Eve get the chance to reveal all of her secrets?
Find out in
THE BRIDE'S SECRETS
by Debra Webb
Available August 2009 from Harlequin Intrigue®

We'll be spotlighting a different series every month throughout 2009 to celebrate our 60th anniversary.

LOOK FOR
HARLEQUIN INTRIGUE®
IN AUGUST!

To commemorate the event, Harlequin Intrigue® is thrilled to invite you to the wedding of the Colby Agency's J.T. Baxley and his bride, Eve Mattson.

Look for *Colby Agency: Elite Reconnaissance*

THE BRIDE'S SECRETS
BY DEBRA WEBB

Available August 2009

www.eHarlequin.com

HIBPA09

CAVANAUGH
JUSTICE

The Cavanaughs are back!

USA TODAY bestselling author

Marie Ferrarella

Cavanaugh Pride

In charge of searching for a serial killer on the loose,
Detective Frank McIntyre has his hands full. When
Detective Julianne White Bear arrives in town searching
for her missing cousin, Frank has to keep the escalating
danger under control while trying to deny the very
real attraction he has for Julianne. Can they keep their
growing feelings under wraps while also handling the
most dangerous case of their careers?

Available August wherever books are sold.

Stay up-to-date on all your romance reading news!

The Inside Romance newsletter is a **FREE** quarterly newsletter highlighting our upcoming series releases and promotions!

Go to
eHarlequin.com/InsideRomance
or e-mail us at
InsideRomance@Harlequin.com
to sign up to receive
your **FREE** newsletter today!

REQUEST YOUR FREE BOOKS!

2 FREE NOVELS PLUS 2 FREE GIFTS!

HARLEQUIN®

Blaze™

Red-hot reads!

YES! Please send me 2 FREE Harlequin® Blaze™ novels and my 2 FREE gifts (gifts are worth about $10). After receiving them, if I don't wish to receive any more books, I can return the shipping statement marked "cancel". If I don't cancel, I will receive 6 brand-new novels every month and be billed just $4.24 per book in the U.S. or $4.71 per book in Canada. That's a savings of 15% off the cover price. It's quite a bargain. Shipping and handling is just 50¢ per book.* I understand that accepting the 2 free books and gifts places me under no obligation to buy anything. I can always return a shipment and cancel at any time. Even if I never buy another book, the two free books and gifts are mine to keep forever.

151 HDN EYS2 351 HDN EYTE

Name	(PLEASE PRINT)	
Address		Apt. #
City	State/Prov.	Zip/Postal Code

Signature (if under 18, a parent or guardian must sign)

Mail to the **Harlequin Reader Service:**
IN U.S.A.: P.O. Box 1867, Buffalo, NY 14240-1867
IN CANADA: P.O. Box 609, Fort Erie, Ontario L2A 5X3

Not valid to current subscribers of Harlequin Blaze books.

Want to try two free books from another line?
Call 1-800-873-8635 or visit www.morefreebooks.com.

* Terms and prices subject to change without notice. Prices do not include applicable taxes. N.Y. residents add applicable sales tax. Canadian residents will be charged applicable provincial taxes and GST. Offer not valid in Quebec. This offer is limited to one order per household. All orders subject to approval. Credit or debit balances in a customer's account(s) may be offset by any other outstanding balance owed by or to the customer. Please allow 4 to 6 weeks for delivery. Offer available while quantities last.

Your Privacy: Harlequin Books is committed to protecting your privacy. Our Privacy Policy is available online at www.eHarlequin.com or upon request from the Reader Service. From time to time we make our lists of customers available to reputable third parties who may have a product or service of interest to you. If you would prefer we not share your name and address, please check here. ☐

HB09R3

COMING NEXT MONTH

Available July 28, 2009

#483 UNBRIDLED Tori Carrington
After being arrested for a crime he didn't commit, former Marine Carter Southard is staying far away from the one thing that's always gotten him into trouble—women! Unfortunately, his sexy new attorney, Laney Cartwright, is making that very difficult....

#484 THE PERSONAL TOUCH Lori Borrill
Professional matchmaker Margot Roth needs to give her latest client the personal touch—property mogul Clint Hilton is a playboy extraordinaire and is looking for a date...for his mother. But while Margot's setting up mom, Clint decides Margot's for him. Let the seduction begin!

#485 HOT UNDER PRESSURE Kathleen O'Reilly
Where You Least Expect It
Ashley Larsen and David McLean are hot for each other. Who knew the airport would be the perfect place to find the perfect sexual partner? But can the lust last when it's a transcontinental journey every time these two want to hook up?

#486 SLIDING INTO HOME Joanne Rock
Encounters
Take me out to the ball game... Four sexy major leaguers are duking it out for the ultimate prize—the Golden Glove award. Little do they guess that the women fate puts in their path will offer them even more of a challenge...and a much more satisfying reward!

#487 STORM WATCH Jill Shalvis
Uniformly Hot!
During his stint in the National Guard, Jason Mauer had seen his share of natural disasters. But when he finds himself in a flash flood with an old crush—sexy Lizzy Mann—the waves of desire turn out to be too much....

#488 THE MIGHTY QUINNS: CALLUM Kate Hoffmann
Quinns Down Under
Gemma Moynihan's sexy Irish eyes are smiling on Callum Quinn! Charming the ladies has never been quiet Cal's style. But he plans to charm the pants off luscious Gemma—until he finds out she's keeping a dangerous secret...

www.eHarlequin.com

HBCNM8PA0709